I0609606

Alfred Tennyson

Poems of Imagination and Fancy

Alfred Tennyson

Poems of Imagination and Fancy

ISBN/EAN: 9783337408282

Printed in Europe, USA, Canada, Australia, Japan

Cover: Foto ©Andreas Hilbeck / pixelio.de

More available books at **www.hansebooks.com**

POEMS

OF

IMAGINATION AND FANCY.

BY

ALFRED TENNYSON,

POET LAUREATE.

ELEGANTLY ILLUSTRATED.

PHILADELPHIA:

PUBLISHED BY E. H. BUTLER & CO.

1865.

Gift
Dr. H. N. Fowler
May 16 1934

ADVERTISEMENT.

ALFRED TENNYSON, like his great predecessor on the Laureate's throne, claims no title but that of poet. His pen has never stooped even to "numerous prose."

In Lotos-eating dreams he murmurs melodious verse. Life with him is a pageant of the Muses. Love rejoices in rhyme, or renders its despair in moaning refrains. Death calls for poetic grief, and inscribes noble verses *In Memoriam* on the urn of the lost.

Such devotion to his art would in itself produce excellence; but his gifts far exceed his acquisitions. He is the most harmonious of the English Poets. We cannot say simply that he adapts the sweet words to the thoughts;—the words are the thoughts: they are instinct with life; paraphrase them and the spell is broken.

Apart from this his descriptive powers are also very great.

Who but Tennyson could, in this age of the real and
useful, have so re-inspired the mythic history of Arthur,
as to charm every reader, awakening our admiration and
pity as though the magnificent prince really armed and
mounted in our presence, and the sinning and repentant
Guinevere stood in her speechless and tearful beauty
before our very eyes?

CONTENTS.

CONTENTS.

POEMS

OF

IMAGINATION AND FANCY.

DEDICATION TO THE QUEEN.

REVERED, beloved,—O you that hold
   A nobler office upon earth
   Than arms, or power of brain, or birth,
Could give the warrior kings of old,

Victoria,—since your Royal grace
   To one of less desert allows
   This laurel greener from the brows
Of him that uttered nothing base;

And should your greatness, and the care
   That yokes with empire, yield you time
   To make demand of modern rhyme,
If aught of ancient worth be there;

Then—while a sweeter music wakes,
   And through wild March the throstle calls,
   Where, all about your palace-walls,
The sunlit almond-blossom shakes—

2 (13)

Take, Madam, this poor book of song;
  For, though the faults were thick as dust
  In vacant chambers, I could trust
Your kindness.   May you rule us long,

And leave us rulers of your blood
  As noble till the latest day !
  May children of our children say,
"She wrought her people lasting good :

" Her court was pure; her life serene;
  God gave her peace; her land reposed,
  A thousand claims to reverence closed
In her as Mother, Wife, and Queen;

" And statesmen at her council met
  Who knew the seasons, when to take
  Occasion by the hand, and make
The bounds of freedom wider yet.

By shaping some august decree.
  Which kept her throne unshaken still
  Broad-based upon her people's will,
And compassed by the inviolate sea."

LILIAN.

Airy, fairy Lilian,
Flitting, fairy Lilian,

LILIAN.

When I ask her if she love me,
Clasps her tiny hands above me,
  Laughing all she can ;
She'll not tell me if she love me,
  Cruel little Lilian.

When my passion seeks
Pleasance in love-sighs,
She, looking through and through me
Thoroughly to undo me,
  Smiling, never speaks :
So innocent-arch, so cunning-simple,
From beneath her gathered wimple
  Glancing with black-beaded eyes,
Till the lightning laughters dimple
  The baby-roses in her cheeks ;
  Then away she flies.

Prithee weep, May Lilian !
  Gayety without eclipse
Wearieth me, May Lilian :
Through my very heart it thrilleth
  When from crimson-threaded lips
Silver-treble laughter trilleth :
  Prithee weep, May Lilian.

Praying all I can,
If prayers will not hush thee,
  Airy Lilian,
Like a rose-leaf I will crush thee,
  Fairy Lilian.

ISABEL.

Eyes not down-dropt nor over-bright, but fed
  With the clear-pointed flame of chastity,
  Clear without heat, undying, tended by
    Pure vestal thoughts in the translucent fane
Of her still spirit; locks not wide dispread,
  Madonna-wise on either side her head;
  Sweet lips whereon perpetually did reign
  The summer calm of golden charity,
Were fixed shadows of thy fixed mood.
  Revered Isabel, the crown and head,
The stately flower of female fortitude,
  Of perfect wifehood and pure lowlihead.

The intuitive decision of a bright
  And thorough-edged intellect to part
    Error from crime; a prudence to withhold;
  The laws of marriage charactered in gold
  Upon the blanched tablets of her heart;
A love still burning upward, giving light
To read those laws; an accent very low
In blandishment, but a most silver flow
  Of subtle-paced counsel in distress,
Right to the heart and brain, though undescried,
  Winning its way with extreme gentleness
Through all the outworks of suspicious pride;
A courage to endure and to obey;
A hate of gossip parlance, and of sway,

Crowned Isabel, through all her placid life,
The queen of marriage, a most perfect wife.

The mellowed reflex of a winter moon ;
A clear stream flowing with a muddy one,
　Till in its onward current it absorbs
　　With swifter movement and in purer light
　　The vexed eddies of its wayward brother.
A leaning and upbearing parasite,
Clothing the stem, which else had fallen quite,
With clustered flower-bells and ambrosial orbs
　Of rich fruit-bunches leaning on each other—
　Shadow forth thee :—the world hath not another
(Though all her fairest forms are types of thee,
And thou of God in thy great charity,)
Of such a finished chastened purity.

MADELINE.

Thou art not steeped in golden languors,
　No tranced summer calm is thine,
　　Ever-varying Madeline.
　Through light and shadow thou dost range,
　Sudden glances, sweet and strange,
Delicious spites, and darling angers,
　And airy forms of flitting change.
Smiling, frowning, evermore,
　Thou art perfect in love-lore.

2 *

Revealings deep and clear are thine
Of wealthy smiles : but who may know
Whether smile or frown be fleeter?
Whether smile or frown be sweeter,
　　Who may know ?

Frowns perfect-sweet along the brow
Light-glooming over eyes divine,
Like little clouds sun-fringed, are thine,
　　Ever-varying Madeline.
Thy smile and frown are not aloof
　　From one another,
　　Each to each is dearest brother;
Hues of the silken sheeny woof
Momently shot into each other.
　　All the mystery is thine ;
Smiling, frowning, evermore,
Thou art perfect in love-lore,
　　Ever-varying Madeline.

A subtle, sudden flame,
　　By veering passion fanned,
　　About thee breaks and dances.
When I would kiss thy hand,
The flush of angered shame
　　O'erflows thy calmer glances,
And o'er black brows drops down
A sudden-curved frown :
But when I turn away,
Thou, willing me to stay,

Wooest not, nor vainly wranglest,
  But, looking fixedly the while,
All my bounding heart entanglest
  In a golden-netted smile;
Then in madness and in bliss,
If my lips should dare to kiss
Thy taper fingers amorously,
Again thou blushest angerly;
And o'er black brows drops down
A sudden-curved frown.

———

A CHARACTER.

With a half-glance upon the sky
At night he said, "The wanderings
Of this most intricate Universe
Teach me the nothingness of things."
Yet could not all creation pierce
Beyond the bottom of his eye.

He spake of beauty: that the dull
Saw no divinity in grass,
Life in dead stones, or spirit in air;
Then looking as 'twere in a glass,
He smoothed his chin and sleeked his hair,
And said the earth was beautiful.

He spake of virtue: not the gods
More purely, when they wish to charm

Pallas and Juno sitting by :
And with a sweeping of the arm,
And a lack-lustre dead-blue eye,
Devolved his rounded periods.

Most delicately hour by hour
He canvassed human mysteries,
And trod on silk, as if the winds
Blew his own praises in his eyes,
And stood aloof from other minds
In impotence of fancied power.

With lips depressed as he were meek,
Himself unto himself he sold :
Upon himself himself did feed :
Quiet, dispassionate, and cold,
And other than his form of creed,
With chiselled features clear and sleek.

THE POET.

THE poet in a golden clime was born,
    With golden stars above;
Dowered with the hate of hate, the scorn of scorn,
    The love of love.

He saw through life and death, through good and ill,
    He saw through his own soul.
The marvel of the everlasting will,
    An open scroll,

Before him lay : with echoing feet he threaded
    The secretest walk of fame :
The viewless arrows of his thoughts were headed
    And winged with flame,

Like Indian reeds blown from his silver tongue,
    And of so fierce a flight,
From Calpe unto Caucasus they sung.
    Filling with light

And vagrant melodies the winds*which bore
    Them earthward till they lit ;
Then, like the arrow-seeds of the field-flower,
    The fruitful wit,

Cleaving, took root, and springing forth anew
    Where'er they fell, behold,
Like to the mother plant in semblance, grew
    A flower all gold,

And bravely furnished all abroad to fling
    The winged shafts of truth,
To throng with stately blooms the breathing spring
    Of Hope and Youth.

So many minds did gird their orbs with beams,
    Though one did fling the fire.
Heaven flowed upon the soul in many dreams
    Of high desire.

Thus truth was multiplied on truth, the world
    Like one great garden showed,

And through the wreaths of floating dark upcurled
    Rare sunrise flowed.

And Freedom reared in that august sunrise
    Her beautiful bold brow,
When rites and forms before his burning eyes
    Melted like snow.

There was no blood upon her maiden robes
    Sunned by those orient skies;
But round about the circles of the globes
    Of her keen eyes

And in her raiment's hem was traced in flame
    WISDOM, a name to shake
All evil dreams of power,—a sacred name.
    And when she spake,

Her words did gather thunder as they ran,
    And as the lightning to the thunder
Which follows it, riving the spirit of man,
    Making earth wonder,

So was their meaning to her words.   No sword
    Of wrath her right arm whirled,
But one poor poet's scroll, and with *his* word
    She shook the world.

THE POET'S MIND.

I.

VEX not thou the poet's mind
    With thy shallow wit:
Vex not thou the poet's mind;
    For thou canst not fathom it.
Clear and bright it should be ever,
Flowing like a crystal river;
Bright as light, and clear as wind.

II.

Dark-browed sophist, come not anear;
    All the place is holy ground;
Hollow smile and frozen sneer
        Come not here.
Holy water will I pour
Into every spicy flower
Of the laurel-shrubs that hedge it around.
The flowers would faint at your cruel cheer.
    In your eye there is death,
    There is frost in your breath
Which would blight the plants.
    Where you stand you cannot hear
        From the groves within
        The wild-bird's din.
In the heart of the garden the merry bird chants,
It would fall to the ground if you came in.

In the middle leaps a fountain
    Like sheet lightning,
    Ever brightening
With a low melodious thunder;
All day and all night it is ever drawn
    From the brain of the purple mountain
    Which stands in the distance yonder:
It springs on a level of bowery lawn,
And the mountain draws it from Heaven above,
And it sings a song of undying love;
And yet, though its voice be so clear and full,
You never would hear it—your ears are so dull;
So keep where you are: you are foul with sin;
It would shrink to the earth if you came in.

THE LADY OF SHALOTT.

PART I.

On either side the river lie
Long fields of barley and of rye,
That clothe the wold and meet the sky;
And through the field the road runs by
        To many-towered Camelot;
And up and down the people go,
Gazing where the lilies blow
Round an island there below,
        The island of Shalott.

Willows whiten, aspens quiver,
Little breezes dusk and shiver
Through the wave that runs for ever
By the island in the river
     Flowing down to Camelot.
Four gray walls, and four gray towers,
Overlook a space of flowers,
And the silent isle embowers
     The Lady of Shalott.

By the margin, willow-veiled,
Slide the heavy barges trailed
By slow horses; and unhailed,
The shallop flitteth silken-sailed,
     Skimming down to Camelot:
But who hath seen her wave her hand
Or at the casement seen her stand?
Or is she known in all the land,
     The Lady of Shalott?

Only reapers, reaping early
In among the bearded barley,
Hear a song that echoes cheerly
From the river winding clearly,
     Down to towered Camelot:
And by the moon the reaper weary,
Piling sheaves in uplands airy,
Listening, whispers " 'Tis the fairy
     Lady of Shalott."

3

PART II.

There she weaves by night and day
A magic web with colors gay.
She has heard a whisper say,
A curse is on her if she stay
    To look down to Camelot.
She knows not what the curse may be,
And so she weaveth steadily,
And little other care hath she,
    The Lady of Shalott.

And moving through a mirror clear
That hangs before her all the year,
Shadow of the world appear.
There she sees the highway near
    Winding down to Camelot;
There the river eddy whirls,
And there the surly village-churls,
And the red cloaks of market-girls,
    Pass onward from Shalott.

Sometimes a troop of damsels glad,
An abbot on an ambling pad,
Sometimes a curly shepherd-lad,
Or long-haired page in crimson clad,
    Goes by to towered Camelot;
And sometimes through the mirror blue
The knights come riding two and two:
She hath no loyal knight and true,
    The Lady of Shalott.

But in her web she still delights
To weave the mirror's magic sights,
For often through the silent nights
A funeral, with plumes and lights,
    And music, went to Camelot :
Or when the moon was overhead,
Came two young lovers lately wed ;
"I am half-sick of shadows," said
    The Lady of Shalott.

PART III.

A bow-shot from her bower-eaves,
He rode between the barley sheaves,
The sun came dazzling through the leaves,
And flamed upon the brazen greaves
    Of bold Sir Lancelot.
A redcross knight for ever kneeled
To a lady in his shield,
That sparkled on the yellow field,
    Beside remote Shalott.

The gemmy bridle glittered free,
Like to some branch of stars we see
Hung in the golden Galaxy.
The bridle bells rang merrily
    As he rode down to Camelot :
And from his blazoned baldric slung
A mighty silver bugle hung,
And as he rode his armor rung,
    Beside remote Shalott.

All in the blue unclouded weather
Thick-jewelled shone the saddle-leather,
The helmet and the helmet-feather
Burned like one burning flame together,
    As he rode down to Camelot.
As often through the purple night,
Below the starry clusters bright,
Some bearded meteor, trailing light,
    Moves over still Shalott.

His broad clear brow in sunlight glowed ;
On burnished hooves his war-horse trode ;
From underneath his hemlet flowed
His coal-black curls as on he rode,
    As he rode down to Camelot.
From the bank and from the river
He flashed into the crystal mirror,
"Tirra lirra," by the river
    Sang Sir Lancelot.

She left the web, she left the loom,
She made three paces through the room,
She saw the water-lily bloom,
She saw the helmet and the plume,
    She looked down to Camelot.
Out flew the web and floated wide ;
The mirror cracked from side to side ;
"The curse is come upon me," cried
    The Lady of Shalott.

PART IV.

In the stormy east-wind straining,
The pale yellow woods were waning,
The broad stream in his banks complaining,
Heavily the low sky raining
    Over towered Camelot ;
Down she came and found a boat
Beneath a willow left afloat,
And round about the prow she wrote
    The Lady of Shalott.

And down the river's dim expanse—
Like some bold seër in a trance,
Seeing all his own mischance—
With a glassy countenance
    Did she look to Camelot.
And at the closing of the day
She loosed the chain, and down she lay ;
The broad stream bore her far away,
    The Lady of Shalott.

Lying, robed in snowy white
That loosely flew to left and right—
The leaves upon her falling light—
Through the noises of the night
    She floated down to Camelot :
And as the boat-head wound among
The willowy hills and fields along,
They heard her singing her last song,
    The Lady of Shalott.

3 *

Heard a carol, mournful, holy,
Chanted loudly, chanted lowly,
Till her blood was frozen slowly,
And her eyes were darkened wholly,
        Turned to towered Camelot ;
For ere she reached upon the tide
The first house by the water-side,
Singing in her song she died,
        The Lady of Shalott.

Under tower and balcony,
By garden-wall and gallery,
A gleaming shape she floated by,
Dead-pale between the houses high,
        Silent into Camelot.
Out upon the wharves they came,
Knight and burgher, lord and dame,
And round the prow they read her name,
        The Lady of Shalott.

Who is this? and what is here?
And in the lighted palace near
Died the sound of royal cheer;
And they crossed themselves for fear,
        All the knights at Camelot:
But Lancelot mused a little space ;
He said, "She has a lovely face ;
God in his mercy lend her grace,
        The Lady of Shalott."

SONGS FROM "THE MILLER'S DAUGHTER."

I.

IT is the miller's daughter,
  And she is grown so dear, so dear,
That I would be the jewel
  That trembles at her ear:
For, hid in ringlets day and night,
I'd touch her neck so warm and white.

And I would be the girdle
  About her dainty, dainty waist,
And her heart would beat against me
  In sorrow and in rest :
And I should know if it beat right,
I'd clasp it round so close and tight.

And I would be the necklace,
  And all day long to fall and rise
Upon her balmy bosom,
  With her laughter or her sighs,
And I would lie so light, so light,
I scarce should be unclasped at night.

II.

LOVE that hath us in the net,
Can he pass, and we forget ?
Many suns arise and set.
Many a chance the years beget.
Love the gift is Love the debt.
          Even so.

Love is hurt with jar and fret.
Love is made a vague regret.
Eyes with idle tears are wet.
Idle habit links us yet.
What is love? for we forget:
Ah, no! no!

THE SISTERS.

We were two daughters of one race:
She was the fairest in the face:
   The wind is blowing in turret and tree.
They were together, and she fell;
Therefore revenge became me well.
   O the Earl was fair to see!

She died: she went to burning flame:
She mixed her ancient blood with shame.
   The wind is howling in turret and tree.
Whole weeks and months, and early and late,
To win his love I lay in wait.
   O the Earl was fair to see!

I made a feast; I bade him come:
I won his love, I brought him home.
   The wind is roaring in turret and tree.
And after supper, in a bed,
Upon my lap he laid his head
   O the Earl was fair to see!

I kissed his eyelids into rest :
His ruddy cheek upon my breast.
  The wind is raging in turret and tree.
I hated him with the hate of hell,
But I loved his beauty passing well.
  O the Earl was fair to see!

I rose up in the silent night :
I made my dagger sharp and bright.
  The wind is raving in turret and tree.
As half-asleep his breath he drew,
Three times I stabbed him through and through.
  O the Earl was fair to see!

I curled and combed his comely head,
He looked so grand when he was dead
  The wind is blowing in turret and tree.
I wrapt his body in the sheet,
And laid him at his mother's feet.
  O the Earl was fair to see!

LADY CLARA VERE DE VERE.

LADY Clara Vere de Vere,
  Of me you shall not win renown ;
You thought to break a country heart
  For pastime, ere you went to town.
At me you smiled, but unbeguiled
  I saw the snare, and I retired :

The daughter of a hundred Earls,
  You are not one to be desired.

Lady Clara Vere de Vere,
  I know you proud to bear your name;
Your pride is yet no mate for mine,
  Too proud to care from whence I came.
Nor would I break for your sweet sake
  A heart that dotes on truer charms.
A simple maiden in her flower
  Is worth a hundred coats-of-arms.

Lady Clara Vere de Vere,
  Some meeker pupil you must find,
For were you queen of all that is,
  I could not stoop to such a mind.
You sought to prove how I could love,
  And my disdain is my reply.
The lion on your old stone gates
  Is not more cold to you than I.

Lady Clara Vere de Vere,
  You put strange memories in my head.
Not thrice your branching limes have blown
  Since I beheld young Laurence dead.
O your sweet eyes, your low replies:
  A great enchantress you may be;
But there was that across his throat
  Which you had hardly cared to see.

Lady Clara Vere de Vere,
　When thus he met his mother's view,
She had the passions of her kind,
　She spake some certain truths of you.
Indeed, I heard one bitter word
　That scarce is fit for you to hear ;
Her manners had not that repose
　Which stamps the caste of Vere de Vere.

Lady Clara Vere de Vere,
　There stands a spectre in your hall :
The guilt of blood is at your door :
　You changed a wholesome heart to gall.
You held your course without remorse,
　To make him trust his modest worth,
And, last, you fixed a vacant stare,
　And slew him with your noble birth.

Trust me, Clara Vere de Vere,
　From yon blue heavens above us bent
The grand old gardener and his wife
　Smile at the claims of long descent.
Howe'er it be, it seems to me,
　'Tis only noble to be good.
Kind hearts are more than coronets,
　And simple faith than Norman blood.

I know you, Clara Vere de Vere :
　You pine among your halls and towers,
The languid light of your proud eyes
　Is wearied of the rolling hours.

In glowing health, with boundless wealth,
   But sickening of a vague disease,
You know so ill to deal with time,
   You needs must play such pranks as these.

Clara, Clara Vere de Vere,
   If Time be heavy on your hands,
Are there no beggars at your gate,
   Nor any poor about your lands?
O! teach the orphan-boy to read,
   Or teach the orphan-girl to sew,
Pray Heaven for a human heart,
   And let the foolish yeoman go.

THE TALKING OAK.

ONCE more the gate behind me falls;
   Once more before my face
I see the mouldered Abbey-walls,
   That stand within the chase.

Beyond the lodge the city lies,
   Beneath its drift of smoke;
And ah! with what delighted eyes
   I turn to yonder oak!

For when my passion first began,
   Ere that which in me burned,
The love that makes me thrice a man,
   Could hope itself returned;

To yonder oak within the field
   I spoke without restraint,
And with a larger faith appealed
   Than Papist unto Saint.

For oft I talked with him apart,
   And told him of my choice,
Until he plagiarized a heart,
   And answered with a voice.

Though what he whispered under Heaven
   None else could understand;
I found him garrulously given,
   A babbler in the land.

But since I heard him make reply
   Is many a weary hour;
'Twere well to question him, and try
   If yet he keeps the power.

Hail, hidden to the knees in fern,
   Broad oak of Sumner-chase,
Whose topmost branches can discern
   The roofs of Sumner-place!

Say thou, whereon I carved her name,
   If ever maid or spouse,
As fair as my Olivia, came
   To rest beneath thy boughs?

"O Walter, I have sheltered here
   Whatever maiden grace

4

The good old Summers, year by year,
    Made ripe in Summer-chase:

"Old Summers, when the monk was fat,
    And, issuing shorn and sleek,
Would twist his girdle tight, and pat
    The girls upon the cheek,

"Ere yet, in scorn of Peter's-pence,
    And numbered bead, and shrift,
Bluff Harry broke into the spence,
    And turned the cowls adrift:

"And I have seen some score of those
    Fresh faces, that would thrive
When his man-minded offset rose
    To chase the deer at five;

"And all that from the town would stroll,
    Till that wild wind made work,
In which the gloomy brewer's soul
    Went by me, like a stork:

"The slight she-slips of loyal blood,
    And others, passing praise,
Strait-laced, but all-too-full in bud
    For puritanic stays:

"And I have shadowed many a group
    Of beauties, that were born
In teacup-times of hood and hoop,
    Or while the patch was worn;

' And, leg and arm with love-knots gay,
　About me leaped and laughed
The modish Cupid of the day,
　And shrilled his tinsel shaft.

" I swear (and else may insects prick
　Each leaf into a gall)
This girl, for whom your heart is sick,
　Is three times worth them all;

" For those and theirs, by Nature's law,
　Have faded long ago;
But in these later springs I saw
　Your own Olivia blow,

" From when she gambolled on the greens,
　A baby-germ, to when
The maiden blossoms of her teens
　Could number five from ten.

" I swear, by leaf, and wind and rain,
　(And hear me with thine ears,)
That, though I circle in the grain
　Five hundred rings of years—

" Yet, since I first could cast a shade,
　Did never creature pass
So slightly, musically made,
　So light upon the grass:

" For as to fairies, that will flit
　To make the greensward fresh,

I hold them exquisitely knit,
But far too spare of flesh."

O, hide thy knotted knees in fern,
And overlook the chase;
And from thy topmost branch discern
The roofs of Summer-place.

But thou, whereon I carved her name,
That oft hast heard my vows,
Declare when last Olivia came
To sport beneath thy boughs.

"O yesterday, you know, the fair
Was holden at the town;
Her father left his good arm-chair,
And rode his hunter down.

"And with him Albert came on his.
I looked at him with joy:
As cowslip unto oxlip is,
So seems she to the boy.

"An hour had passed—and, sitting straight
Within the low-wheeled chaise,
Her mother trundled to the gate
Behind the dappled grays.

"But, as for her, she stayed at home,
And on the roof she went,
And down the way you use to come
She looked with discontent.

"She left the novel half-uncut
  Upon the rosewood shelf;
She left the new piano shut :
  She could not please herself.

"Then ran she, gamesome as the colt,
  And livelier than a lark
She sent her voice through all the holt
  Before her, and the park.

"A light wind chased her on the wing,
  And in the chase grew wild,
As close as might be would he cling
  About the darling child :

"But light as any wind that blows
  So fleetly did she stir,
The flower, she touched on, dipped and rose,
  And turned to look at her.

"And here she came, and round me played,
  And sang to me the whole
Of those three stanzas that you made
  About my ' giant bole ;'

"And in a fit of frolic mirth
  She strove to span my waist :
Alas, I was so broad of girth,
  I could not be embraced.

"I wished myself the fair young beech
  That here beside me stands,

4*

That round me, clasping each in each,
    She might have locked her hands.

" Yet seemed the pressure thrice as sweet
    As woodbine's fragile hold,
Or when I feel about my feet
    The berried briony fold."

O muffle round thy knees with fern,
    And shadow Sumner-chase!
Long may thy topmost branch discern
    The roofs of Sumner-place!

But tell me, did she read the name
    I carved with many vows,
When last with throbbing heart I came
    To rest beneath thy boughs ?

"O yes, she wandered round and round
    These knotted knees of mine,
And found, and kissed the name she found.
    And sweetly murmured thine.

" A tear-drop trembled from its source,
    And down my surface crept.
My sense of touch is something coarse,
    But I believe she wept.

"Then flushed her cheek with rosy light,
    She glanced across the plain ;
But not a creature was in sight :
    She kissed me once again.

"Her kisses were so close and kind,
    That, trust me on my word,
Hard wood I am, and wrinkled rind,
    But yet my sap was stirred :

"And even into my inmost ring
    A pleasure I discerned,
Like those blind motions of the Spring,
    That show the year is turned.

"Thrice-happy he that may caress
    The ringlet's waving balm—
The cushions of whose touch may press
    The maiden's tender palm.

"I, rooted here among the groves,
    But languidly adjust
My vapid vegetable loves
    With anthers and with dust :

"For ah ! my friend, the days were brief
    Whereof the poets talk,
When that, which breathes within the leaf,
    Could slip its bark and walk.

"But could I, as in times foregone,
    From spray, and branch, and stem
Have sucked and gathered into one
    The life that spreads in them,

"She had not found me so remiss ;
    But lightly issuing through,

I would have paid her kiss for kiss
  With usury thereto."

O flourish high, with leafy towers,
  And overlook the lea,
Pursue thy loves among the bowers,
  But leave thou mine to me.

O flourish, hidden deep in fern,
  Old oak, I love thee well;
A thousand thanks for what I learn
  And what remains to tell.

" 'Tis little more: the day was warm;
  At last, tired out with play,
She sank her head upon her arm,
  And at my feet she lay.

" Her eyelids dropped their silken eaves;
  I breathed upon her eyes
Through all the summer of my leaves
  A welcome mixed with sighs.

" I took the swarming sound of life—
  The music from the town—
The murmurs of the drum and fife,
  And lulled them in my own.

" Sometimes I let a sunbeam slip,
  To light her shaded eye;
A second fluttered round her lip
  Like a golden butterfly;

"A thid would glimmer on her neck
    To make the necklace shine;
Another slid, a sunny fleck,
    From head to ankle fine.

"Then close and dark my arms I spread,
    And shadowed all her rest—
Dropped dews upon her golden head,
    An acorn in her breast.

"But in a pet she started up,
    And plucked it out, and drew
My little oakling from the cup,
    And flung him in the dew.

"And yet it was a graceful gift—
    I felt a pang within
As when I see the woodman lift
    His axe to slay my kin.

"I shook him down because he was
    The finest on the tree.
He lies beside thee on the grass.
    O kiss him once for me!

"O kiss him twice and thrice for me,
    That have no lips to kiss,
For never yet was oak on lea
    Shall grow so fair as this."

Step deeper yet in herb and fern,
    Look further through the chase,

Spread upward till thy boughs discern
   The front of Sumner-place.

This fruit of thine by Love is blest,.
   That but a moment lay
Where fairer fruit of Love may rest
   Some happy future day.

I kiss it twice, I kiss it thrice,
   The warmth it thence shall win
To riper life may magnetize
   The baby-oak within.

But thou, while kingdoms overset,
   Or lapse from hand to hand,
Thy leaf shall never fail, nor yet
   Thine acorn in the land.

May never saw dismember thee,
   Nor wielded axe disjoint;
That art the fairest spoken tree
   From here to Lizard-point.

O rock upon thy towery top
   All throats that gurgle sweet!
All starry culmination drop
   Balm-dews to bathe thy feet!

All grass of silky feather grow—
   And while he sinks or swells
The full south-breeze around thee blow
   The sound of minster bells.

The fat earth feed thy branchy root,
    That under deeply strikes!
The northern morning o'er thee shoot,
    High up, in silver spikes!

Nor ever lightning char thy grain,
    But, rolling as in sleep,
Low thunders bring the mellow rain,
    That makes thee broad and deep!

And hear me swear a solemn oath,
    That only by thy side
Will I to Olive plight my troth,
    And gain her for my bride.

And when my marriage-morn may fall,
    She, Dryad-like, shall wear
Alternate leaf and acorn-ball
    In wreath about her hair.

And I will work in prose and rhyme,
    And praise thee more in both
Than bard has honored beech or lime,
    Or that Thessalian growth

In which the swarthy ringdove sat,
    And mystic sentence spoke;
And more than England honors that,
    Thy famous brother-oak,

Wherein the younger Charles abode
    Till all the paths were dim,

And far below the Roundhead rode,
And hummed a surly hymn.

THE MAY QUEEN.

You must wake and call me early, call me early, mother dear;
To-morrow 'ill be the happiest time of all the glad New-year;
Of all the glad New-year, mother, the maddest, merriest day;
For I'm to be Queen o' the May, mother, I'm to be Queen o' the
May.

There's many a black, black eye, they say, but none so bright as
mine;
There's Margaret and Mary, there's Kate and Caroline:
But none so fair as little Alice in all the land, they say:
So I'm to be Queen o' the May, mother, I'm to be Queen o' the
May.

I sleep so sound all night, mother, that I shall never wake,
If you do not call me loud when the day begins to break:
But I must gather knots of flowers, and buds and garlands gay,
For I'm to be Queen o' the May, mother, I'm to be Queen o' the
May.

As I came up the valley, whom think ye should I see,
But Robin leaning on the bridge beneath the hazel-tree?
He thought of that sharp look, mother, I gave him yesterday,—
But I'm to be Queen o' the May, mother, I'm to be Queen o' the
May.

He thought I was a ghost, mother, for I was all in white,
And I ran by him without speaking, like a flash of light.
They call me cruel-hearted, but I care not what they say,
For I'm to be Queen o' the May, mother, I'm to be Queen o' the
  • May.

They say he's dying all for love, but that can never be:
They say his heart is breaking, mother—what is that to me?
There's many a bolder lad 'ill woo me any summer day,
And I'm to be Queen o' the May, mother, I'm to be Queen o'
    the May.

Little Effie shall go with me to-morrow to the green,
And you'll be there, too, mother, to see me made the Queen:
For the shepherd lads on every side 'ill come from far away,
And I'm to be Queen o' the May, mother, I'm to be Queen o'
    the May.

The honeysuckle round the porch has woven its wavy bowers,
And by the meadow-trenches blow the faint sweet cuckoo-flowers;
And the wild marsh-marigold shines like fire in swamps and
    hollows gray,
And I'm to be Queen o' the May, mother, I'm to be Queen o'
    the May.

The night-winds come and go, mother, upon the meadow grass,
And the happy stars above them seem to brighten as they pass;
There will not be a drop of rain the whole of the livelong day,
And I'm to be Queen o' the May, mother, I'm to be Queen o'
    the May.
    5

All the valley, mother, 'ill be fresh and green and still,
And the cowslip and the crowfoot are over all the hill,
And the rivulet in the flowery dale 'ill merrily glance and play,
For I'm to be Queen o' the May, mother, I'm to be Queen o' the
   May.

So you must wake and call me early, call me early, mother dear,
To-morrow 'ill be the happiest time of all the glad New-year:
To-morrow 'ill be of all the year the maddest, merriest day,
For I'm to be Queen o' the May, mother, I'm to be Queen o' the
   May.

NEW YEAR'S EVE.

If you're waking call me early, call me early, mother dear,
For I would see the sun rise upon the glad New-year.
It is the last New-year that I shall ever see,
Then you may lay me low i' the mould, and think no more of me.

To-night I saw the sun set: he set and left behind
The good old year, the dear old time, and all my peace of mind;
And the New-year's coming up, mother, but I shall never see
The blossom on the blackthorn, the leaf upon the tree.

Last May we made a crown of flowers: we had a merry day;
Beneath the hawthorn on the green they made me Queen of May;
And we danced about the May-pole and in the hazel copse,
Till Charles's Wain came out above the tall white chimney-tops.

There's not a flower on all the hills: the frost is on the pane:
I only wish to live till the snowdrops come again:

I wish the snow would melt and the sun come out on high:
I long to see a flower so before the day I die.

The building rook 'ill caw from the windy tall elm-tree,
And the tufted plover pipe along the fallow lea,
And the swallow 'ill come back again with summer o'er the wave
But I shall lie alone, mother, within the mouldering grave.

Upon the chancel-casement, and upon that grave of mine,
In the early early morning the summer sun 'ill shine,
Before the red cock crows from the farm upon the hill,
When you are warm-asleep, mother, and all the world is still.

When the flowers come again, mother, beneath the waning light
You'll never see me more in the long gray fields at night;
When from the dry dark wold the summer airs blow cool
On the oat-grass and the sword-grass, and the bulrush in the pool.

You'll bury me, my mother, just beneath the hawthorn shade,
And you'll come sometimes and see me where I am lowly laid.
I shall not forget you mother, I shall hear you when you pass,
With your feet above my head in the long and pleasant grass.

I have been wild and wayward, but you'll forgive me now ;
You'll kiss me, my own mother, and forgive me ere I go :
Nay, nay, you must not weep, nor let your grief be wild,
You should not fret for me, mother, you have another child.

If I can. I'll come again, mother, from out my resting-place;
Though you'll not see me, mother, I shall look upon your face ;
Though I cannot speak a word, I shall harken what you say,
And be often, often with you when you think I'm far away.

Good-night, good-night, when I have said good-night for evermore,
And you see me carried out from the threshold of the door ;
Don't let Effie come to see me till my grave be growing green :
She'll be a better child to you than ever I have been.

She'll find my garden-tools upon the granary floor :
Let her take 'em : they are hers : I shall never garden more :
But tell her, when I'm gone, to train the rose-bush that I set
About the parlor-window and the box of mignonette.

Good-night, sweet mother : call me before the day is born.
All night I lie awake, but I fall asleep at morn ;
But I would see the sun rise upon the glad New-year,
So, if you're waking, call me, call me early, mother dear.

CONCLUSION.

I THOUGHT to pass away before, and yet alive I am ;
And in the fields all round I hear the bleating of the lamb.
How sadly, I remember, rose the morning of the year !
To die before the snowdrop came, and now the violet's here.

O sweet is the new violet, that comes beneath the skies,
And sweeter is the young lamb's voice to me that cannot rise,
And sweet is all the land about, and all the flowers that blow,
And sweeter far is death than life to me that long to go.

It seemed so hard at first, mother, to leave the blessed sun,
And now it seems as hard to say ; and yet, His will be done !
But still I think it can't be long before I find release ;
And that good man, the clergyman, has told me words of peace.

O blessings on his kindly voice and on his silver hair!
And blessings on his whole life long, until he meet me there!
O blessings on his kindly heart and on his silver head!
A thousand times I blessed him, as he knelt beside my bed.

He taught me all the mercy, for he showed me all the sin.
Now, though my lamp was lighted late, there's One will let me in:
Nor would I now be well, mother, again, if that could be,
For my desire is but to pass to Him that died for me

I did not hear the dog howl, mother, or the deathwatch beat,
There came a sweeter token when the night and morning meet:
But sit beside my bed, mother, and put your hand in mine,
And Effie on the other side, and I will tell the sign.

All in the wild March-morning I heard the angels call;
It was when the moon was setting, and the dark was over all;
The trees began to whisper, and the wind began to roll,
And in the wild March-morning I heard them call my soul.

For lying broad awake I thought of you and Effie dear;
I saw you sitting in the house, and I no longer here;
With all my strength I prayed for both, and so I felt resigned,
And up the valley came a swell of music on the wind.

I thought that it was fancy, and I listened in my bed,
And then did something speak to me—I know not what was said;
For great delight and shuddering took hold of all my mind,
And up the valley came again the music on the wind.

5 *

But you were sleeping; and I said, " It's not for them; it's mine."
And if it comes three times, I thought, I take it for a sign.
And once again it came, and close beside the window-bars,
Then seemed to go right up to heaven and die among the stars.

So now I think my time is near. I trust it is. I know
The blessed music went that way my soul will have to go.
And for myself, indeed, I care not if I go to-day,
But, Effie, you must comfort *her* when I am passed away.

And say to Robin a kind word, and tell him not to fret;
There's many worthier than I would make him happy yet.
If I had lived—I cannot tell—I might have been his wife;
But all these things have ceased to be, with my desire of life.

O look! the sun begins to rise, the heavens are in a glow;
He shines upon a hundred fields, and all of them I know.
And there I move no longer now, and there his light may shine—
Wild flowers in the valley for other hands than mine.

O sweet and strange it seems to me, that ere this day is done
The voice that now is speaking may be beyond the sun—
For ever and for ever with those just souls and true—
And what is life, that we should moan? why make we such ado?

For ever and for ever, all in a blessed home—
And there to wait a little while till you and Effie come—
To lie within the light of God, as I lie upon your breast—
And the wicked cease from troubling, and the weary are at rest.

BREAK, BREAK, BREAK.

BREAK, break, break,
  On thy cold gray stones, oh Sea!
And I would that my tongue could utter '
  The thoughts that arise in me.

O well for the fisherman's boy,
  That he shouts with his sister at play!
O well for the sailor lad,
  That he sings in his boat on the bay!

And the stately ships go on
  To their haven under the hill;
But oh for the touch of a vanished hand,
  And the sound of a voice that is still!

Break, break, break,
  At the foot of thy crags, oh Sea!
But the tender grace of a day that is dead
  Will never come back to me.

THE DEATH OF THE OLD YEAR.

FULL knee-deep lies the winter snow,
And the winter winds are wearily sighing:
Toll ye the church-bell sad and slow,
And tread softly and speak low,
For the old year lies a-dying.

Old year, you must not die;
You came to us so readily,
You lived with us so steadily,
Old year, you shall not die.

He lieth still: he doth not move :
He will not see the dawn of day.
He hath no other life above.
He gave me a friend, and a true, true-love,
And the New-year will take 'em away.
Old year, you must not go ;
So long as you have been with us,
Such joy as you have seen with us,
Old year, you shall not go.

He frothed his bumpers to the brim;
A jollier year we shall not see.
But though his eyes are waxing dim,
And though his foes speak ill of him,
He was a friend to me.
Old year, you shall not die;
We did so laugh and cry with you,
I've half a mind to die with you,
Old year, if you must die.

He was full of joke and jest,
But all his merry quips are o'er.
To see him die, across the waste
His son and heir doth ride post-haste,
But he'll be dead before.

Every one for his own.
The night is starry and cold, my friend,
And the New-year, blithe and bold, my friend,
Comes up to take his own.

How hard he breathes! over the snow
I heard just now the crowing cock
The shadows flicker to and fro :
The cricket chirps : the light burns low :
'Tis nearly twelve o'clock.
    Shake hands, before you die.
    Old year, we'll dearly rue for you :
    What is it we can do for you?
    Speak out before you die.

His face is growing sharp and thin.
Alack ! our friend is gone.
Close up his eyes : tie up his chin :
Step from the corpse, and let him in
That standeth there alone,
    And waiteth at the door.
    There's a new foot on the floor, my friend,
    And a new face at the door, my friend,
    A new face at the door.

THE BROOK.

AN IDYL.

" HERE, by this brook, we parted; I to the East,
And he for Italy—too late—too late:
One whom the strong sons of the world despise;
For lucky rhymes to him were scrip and snare,
And mellow metres more than cent. for cent.;
Nor could he understand how money breeds,
Thought it a dead thing; yet himself could make
The thing that is not as the thing it is.
O had he lived! In our school-books we say,
Of those that held their heads above the crowd,
They flourished then or then; but life in him
Could scarce be said to flourish, only touched
On such a time as goes before the leaf,
When all the wood stands in a mist of green,
And nothing perfect: yet the brook he loved,
For which, in branding summers of Bengal,
Or even the sweet half-English Neilgherry air,
I panted, seems, as I re-listen to it,
Prattling the primrose fancies of the boy,
To me that loved him; for 'O brook,' he says,
'O babbling brook,' says Edmund in his rhyme,
'Whence come you?' and the brook, why not? replies.

> I come from haunts of coot and hern,
>   I make a sudden sally
> And sparkle out among the fern,
>   To bicker down a valley.

By thirty hills I hurry down,
 Or slip between the ridges,
By twenty thorps, a little town,
 And half a hundred bridges.

Till last by Philip's farm I flow
 To join the brimming river,
For men may come and men may go,
 But I go on for ever.

"Poor lad, he died at Florence, quite worn out,
Travelling to Naples. There is Darnley bridge,
It has more ivy; there the river; and there
Stands Philip's farm where brook and river meet.

I chatter over stony ways,
 In little sharps and trebles,
I bubble into eddying bays,
 I babble on the pebbles.

With many a curve my banks I fret
 By many a field and fallow,
And many a fairy foreland set
 With willow-weed and mallow.

I chatter, chatter, as I flow
 To join the brimming river,
For men may come and men may go,
 But I go on for ever.

"But Philip chattered more than brook or bird;
Old Philip; all about the fields you caught
His weary daylong chirping, like the dry
High-elbowed grigs that leap in summer grass.

I wind about, and in and out,
  With here a blossom sailing,
And here and there a lusty trout,
  And here and there a grayling,

And here and there a foamy flake
  Upon me, as I travel,
With many a silvery waterbreak
  Above the golden gravel,

And draw them all along, and flow
  To join the brimming river,
For men may come and men may go,
  But I go on for ever.

"O darling Katie Willows, his one child!
A maiden of our century, yet most meek;
A daughter of our meadows, yet not coarse;
Straight, but as lissome as a hazel wand;
Her eyes a bashful azure, and her hair
In gloss and hue the chestnut, when the shell
Divides threefold to show the fruit within.

"Sweet Katie, once I did her a good turn,
Her and her far-off cousin and betrothed,
James Willows, of one name and heart with her.
For here I came, twenty years back—the week
Before I parted with poor Edmund; crossed
By that old bridge which, half in ruins then,
Still makes a hoary eyebrow for the gleam
Beyond it, where the waters marry—crossed,

Whistling a random bar of Bonny Doon,
And pushed at Philip's garden-gate. The gate,
Half-parted from a weak and scolding hinge,
Stuck; and he clamored from a casement, 'run,'
To Katie somewhere in the walks below,
'Run, Katie!' Katie never ran : she moved
To meet me, winding under woodbine bowers,
A little fluttered, with her eyelids down,
Fresh apple-blossom, blushing for a boon.

"What was it? less of sentiment than sense
Had Katie; not illiterate; neither one
Who dabbling in the fount of fictive tears,
And nursed by mealy-mouthed philanthropies,
Divorce the Feeling from her mate the Deed.

"She told me. She and James had quarrelled.
What cause of quarrel? None, she said, no cause;
James had no cause : but when I pressed the cause,
I learnt that James had flickering jealousies
Which angered her. Who angered James? I said.
But Katie snatched her eyes at once from mine,
And sketching with her slender pointed foot
Some figure like a wizard's pentagram
On garden gravel, let my query pass
Unclaimed, in flushing silence, till I asked
If James were coming. 'Coming every day,'
She answered, 'ever longing to explain,
But evermore her father came across

6

With some long-winded tale, and broke him short;
And James departed vexed with him and her.'
How could I help her?   ' Would I—was it wrong?'
(Clasped hands and that petitionary grace
Of sweet seventeen subdued me ere she spoke)
' O would I take her father for one hour,
For one half-hour, and let him talk to me!'
And even while she spoke, I saw where James
Made toward us, like a wader in the surf,
Beyond the brook, waist-deep in meadow-sweet.

"O Katie, what I suffered for your sake!
For in I went, and called old Philip out
To show the farm : full willingly he rose :
He led me through the short sweet-smelling lanes
Of his wheat-suburb, babbling as he went
He praised his land, his horses, his machines ;
He praised his ploughs, his cows, his hogs, his dogs ;
He praised his hens, his geese, his guinea-hens ;
His pigeons, who in session on their roofs
Approved him, bowing at their own deserts :
Then from the plaintive mother's teat he took
Her blind and shuddering puppies, naming each.
And naming those, his friends, for whom they were :
Then crossed the common into Darnley chase
To show Sir Arthur's deer.   In copse and fern
Twinkled the innumerable ear and tail.
Then, seated on a serpent-rooted beech,

He pointed out a pasturing colt, and said :
' That was the four-year-old I sold the Squire.'
And there he told a long long-winded tale
Of how the Squire had seen the colt at grass,
And how it was the thing his daughter wished,
And how he sent the bailiff to the farm
To learn the price, and what the price he asked,
And how the bailiff swore that he was mad,
But he stood firm ; and so the matter hung ;
He gave them line : and five days after that
He met the bailiff at the Golden Fleece,
Who then and there had offered something more,
But he stood firm ; and so the matter hung ;
He knew the man ; the colt would fetch its price ;
He gave them line : and how by chance at last
(It might be May or April, he forgot,
The last of April or the first of May)
He found the bailiff riding by the farm,
And, talking from the point, he drew him in,
And there he mellowed all his heart with ale,
Until they closed a bargain, hand in hand.

  "Then, while I breathed in sight of haven, he,
Poor fellow, could he help it? recommenced,
And ran through all the coltish chronicle,
Wild Will, Black Bess, Tantivy, Tallyho,
Reform, White Rose, Bellerophon, the Jilt,
Arbaces, and Phenomenon, and the rest,

Till, not to die a listener, I arose,
And with me Philip, talking still; and so
We turned our foreheads from the falling sun,
And following our own shadows thrice as long
As when they followed us from Philip's door,
Arrived, and found the sun of sweet content
Re-risen in Katie's eyes, and all things well.

> I steal by lawns and grassy plots,
>   I slide by hazel covers;
> I move the sweet forget-me-nots
>   That grow for happy lovers.
>
> I slip, I slide, I gloom, I glance,
>   Among my skimming swallows;
> I make the netted sunbeam dance
>   Against my sandy shallows.
>
> I murmur under moon and stars
>   In brambly wildernesses;
> I linger by my shingly bars;
>   I loiter round my cresses;
>
> And out again I curve and flow
>   To join the brimming river,
> For men may come and men may go,
>   But I go on for ever.

Yes, men may come again and go; and these are gone,
All gone. My dearest, brother Edmund, sleeps,
Not by the well-known stream and rustic spire,
But unfamiliar Arno, and the dome

Of Brunelleschi; sleeps in peace: and he,
Poor Philip, of all his lavish waste of words
Remains the lean P. W. on his tomb:
I scraped the lichen from it: Katie walks
By the long wash of Australasian seas
Far off, and holds her head to other stars,
And breathes in converse seasons. All are gone.
  So Lawrence Aylmer, seated on a stile
In the long hedge, and rolling in his mind   •
Old waifs of rhyme, and bowing o'er the brook
A tonsored head in middle age forlorn,
Mused, and was mute. On a sudden a low breath
Of tender air made tremble in the hedge
The fragile bindweed-bells and briony rings;
And he looked up. There stood a maiden near,
Waiting to pass. In much amaze he stared
On eyes a bashful azure, and on hair
In gloss and hue the chestnut, when the shell
Divides threefold to show the fruit within:
Then, wondering, asked her, "Are you from the farm?"—
"Yes," answered she.—"Pray stay a little: pardon me;
What do they call you?"—"Katie."—"That were strange.
What surname?"—"Willows."—"No!"—"That is my
    name."—
"Indeed!" and here he looked so self-perplexed,
That Katie laughed, and laughing blushed, till he
Laughed also, but as one before he wakes,
Who feels a glimmering strangeness in his dream.
  6 *

Then looking at her; ' Too happy, fresh and fair,
Too fresh and fair in our sad world's best bloom,
To be the ghost of one who bore your name
About these meadows, twenty years ago."

" Have you not heard?" said Katie, " We came back.
We bought the farm we tenanted before.
Am I so like her? so they said on board.
Sir, if you knew her in her English days,
My mother, as it seems you did, the days
That most she loves to talk of, come with me.
My brother James is in the harvest-field :
But she—you will be welcome—O, come in !

THE LOTOS-EATERS.

" Courage !" he said, and pointed toward the land ;
"This mounting wave will roll us shoreward soon."
In the afternoon they came unto a land,
In which it seemed always afternoon.
All round the coast the languil air did swoon,
Breathing like one that hath a weary dream.
Full-faced above the valley stood the moon ;
And like a downward smoke, the slender stream
Along the cliff to fall and pause and fall did seem.

A land of streams ! some, like a downward smoke,
Slow-drooping veils of thinnest lawn, did go ;

And some through wavering lights and shadows broke
Rolling a slumbrous sheet of foam below.
They saw the gleaming river seaward flow
From the inner land : far-off, three mountain-tops,
Three silent pinnacles of aged snow,
Stood sunset-flushed : and, dewed with showery drops,
Up-clomb the shadowy pine above the woven copse.

The charmed sunset lingered low adown
In the red West : through mountain clefts the dale
Was seen far inland, and the yellow down
Bordered with palm, and many a winding vale
And meadow, set with slender galingale ;
A land where all things always seemed the same !
And round about the keel with faces pale,
Dark faces pale against that rosy flame,
The mild-eyed melancholy Lotos-eaters came.

Branches they bore of that enchanted stem,
Laden with flower and fruit, whereof they gave
To each, but whoso did receive of them,
And taste, to him the gushing of the wave
Far, far away did seem to mourn and rave
On alien shores ; and if his fellow spake,
His voice was thin, as voices from the grave ;
And deep-asleep he seemed, yet all awake,
And music in his ears his beating heart did make.

They sat them down upon the yellow sand,
Between the sun and moon upon the shore ;

And sweet t was to dream of Father-land,
Of child, and wife, and slave; but evermore
Most weary seemed the sea, weary the oar,
Weary the wandering fields of barren foam.
Then some one said, "We will return no more;
And all at once they sang, "Our island home
Is far beyond the wave; we will no longer roam."

CHORIC SONG.

There is sweet music here that softer falls
Than petals from blown roses on the grass,
Or night-dews on still waters between walls
Of shadowy granite, in a gleaming pass;
Music that gentlier on the spirit lies
Than tired eyelids upon tired eyes;
Music that brings sweet sleep down from the blissful skies.
Here are cool mosses deep,
And through the moss the ivies creep,
And in the stream the long-leaved flowers weep,
And from the craggy ledge the poppy hangs in sleep.

Why are we weighed upon with heaviness,
And utterly consumed with sharp distress,
While all things else have rest from weariness?
All things have rest: why should we toil alone,
We only toil, who are the first of things,
And make perpetual moan,
Still from one sorrow to another thrown:

Nor ever fold our wings,
And cease from wanderings,
Nor steep our brows in slumber's holy balm ;
Nor hearken what the inner spirit sings,
"There is no joy but calm !"
Why should we only toil, the roof and crown of things?

Lo! in the middle of the wood,
The folded leaf is wooed from out the bud
With winds upon the branch, and there
Grows green and broad, and takes no care,
Sun-steeped at noon, and in the moon
Nightly dew-fed ; and turning yellow
Falls and floats adown the air.
Lo! sweetened with the summer light,
The full-juiced apple, waxing over-mellow,
Drops in a silent autumn night.
All its allotted length of days,
The flower ripens in its place,
Ripens and fades, and falls, and hath no toil,
Fast-rooted in the fru'tful soil.

Hateful is the dark-blue sky,
Vaulted o'er the dark-blue sea.
Death is the end of life ; ah, why
Should life all labor be ?
Let us alone.   Time driveth onward fast,
And in a little while our lips are dumb.

Let us alone. What is it that will last?
All things are taken from us, and become
Portions and parcels of the dreadful Past.
Let us alone. What pleasure can we have
To war with evil? Is there any peace
In ever climbing up the climbing wave?
All things have rest, and ripen toward the grave
In silence; ripen, fall and cease:
Give us long rest or death, dark death or dreamful ease!

How sweet it were, hearing the downward stream
With half-shut eyes ever to seem
Falling asleep in a half-dream!
To dream and dream, like yonder amber light,
Which will not leave the myrrh-bush on the height
To hear each other's whispered speech;
Eating the Lotos, day by day,
To watch the crisping ripples on the beach,
And tender-curving lines of creamy spray:
To lend our hearts and spirits wholly
To the influence of mild-minded melancholy;
To muse and brood and live again in memory,
With those old faces of our infancy
Heaped over with a mound of grass,
Two handfuls of white dust, shut in an urn of brass!

Dear is the memory of our wedded lives,
And dear the last embraces of our wives

And their warm tears : but all hath suffered change ;
For surely now our household hearths are cold :
Our sons inherit us : our looks are strange :
And we should come like ghosts to trouble joy.
Or else the island princes, over-bold
Have eat our substance, and the minstrel sings
Before them of the ten-years' war in Troy,
And our great deeds, as half-forgotten things.
Is there confusion in the little isle?
Let what is broken so remain.
The Gods are hard to reconcile :
'Tis hard to settle order once again.
There *is* confusion worse than death,
Trouble on trouble, pain on pain,
Long labor unto aged breath,
Sore task to hearts worn out with many wars,
And eyes grown dim with gazing on the pilot-stars.

But, propped on beds of amaranth and moly,
How sweet (while warm airs lull us, blowing lowly,)
With half-dropped eyelids still,
Beneath a heaven dark and holy,
To watch the long bright river drawing slowly
His waters from the purple hill—
To hear the dewy echoes calling
From cave to cave through the thick-twined vine—
To watch the emerald-colored water falling
Through many a woven acanthus-wreath divine !

Only to hear and see the far-off sparkling brine,
Only to hear were sweet, stretched out beneath the pine.

The Lotos blooms below the barren peak :
The Lotos blows by every winding creek :
All day the wind breathes low with mellower tone ;
Through every hollow cave and alley lone
Round and round the spicy downs the yellow Lotos-dust is blown.
We have had enough of action, and of motion we,
Rolled to starboard, rolled to larboard, when the surge was seeth-
    ing free,
Where the wallowing monster spouted his foam-fountains in the
    sea.
Let us swear an oath, and keep it with an equal mind,
In the hollow Lotos-land to live and lie reclined
On the hills like Gods together, careless of mankind.
For they lie beside their nectar, and the bolts are hurled
Far below them in the valleys, and the clouds are lightly curled
Round their golden houses, girdled with the gleaming world :
Where they smile in secret, looking over wasted lands,
Blight and famine, plague and earthquake, roaring deeps and fiery
    sands,
Clanging fights, and flaming towns, and sinking ships, and pray-
    ing hands.
But they smile, they find a music centred in a doleful song
Steaming up, a lamentation and an ancient tale of wrong,
Like a tale of little meaning, though the words are strong :
Chanted from an ill-used race of men that cleave the soil,

Sow the seed, and reap the harvest with enduring toil,
Storing yearly little dues of wheat, and wine and oil;
Till they perish and they suffer—some, 'tis whispered—down in
    hell
Suffer endless anguish, others in Elysian valleys dwell,
Resting weary limbs at last on beds of asphodel.
Surely, surely, slumber is more sweet than toil, the shore
Than labor in the deep mid-ocean, wind and wave and oar;
O rest ye, brother mariners, we will not wander more.

TO GARIBALDI.

TRUE thinker and true worker, hand in hand,
    Unlike, but yet how like each bears his part;
    Hero and poet with the same great heart.
In one the life-blood of the southern land
    Pulses with sudden throb, as beat the waves
    Where the blue sea his rocky islet laves;
The other, master of the mighty rhyme,
Had pierced the dusky mantle of past time,
    And seen the shadows of the noble dead,
    The knightly throng, with Arthur at their head,
Writing their Idyls in a deathless song:
    Deeming, perchance, such life a dim ideal—
Its gentle strength, its fearless scorn of wrong—
    On Garibaldi gazed, and found it real.

7

THE

CHARGE OF THE LIGHT BRIGADE.

HALF a league, half a league,
  Half a league onward,
All in the valley of Death
  Rode the six hundred.
" Forward, the Light Brigade !
" Charge for the guns !" he said :
Into the valley of Death
  Rode the six hundred.

" Forward, the Light Brigade !"
Was there a man dismayed ?
Not though the soldier knew
  Some one had blundered :
Theirs not to make reply,
Theirs not to reason why,
Theirs but to do and die,
Into the valley of Death
  Rode the six hundred.

Cannon to right of them,
Cannon to left of them,
Cannon in front of them
  Volleyed and thundered ;
Stormed at with shot and shell,
Boldly they rode and well,

Into the jaws of Death,
Into the mouth of Hell
 Rode the six hundred.

Flashed all their sabres bare,
Flashed as they turned in air,
Sabring the gunners there,
Charging an army, while
 All the world wondered :
Plunged in the battery-smoke
Right through the line they broke;
Cossack and Russian
Reeled from the sabre-stroke
 Shattered and sundered.
· Then they rode back, but not
 Not the six hundred.

Cannon to right of them,
Cannon to left of them,
Cannon behind them
 Volleyed and thundered ;
Stormed at with shot and shell,
While horse and hero fell,
They that had fought so well
Came through the jaws of Death
Back from the mouth of Hell,
All that was left of them,
 Left of six hundred.

When can their glory fade?
O the wild charge they made!
All the world wondered.
Honor the charge they made!
Honor the Light Brigade,
Noble six hundred!

———

MORTE D'ARTHUR.

So all day long the noise of battle rolled
Among the mountains by the winter sea;
Until King Arthur's table, man by man,
Had fallen in Lyonness about their Lord.
King Arthur: then, because his wound was deep,
The bold Sir Bedivere uplifted him,
Sir Bedivere, the last of all his knights,
And bore him to a chapel nigh the field,
A broken chancel with a broken cross,
That stood on a dark strait of barren land.
On one side lay the Ocean, and on one
Lay a great water, and the moon was full.
    Then spake King Arthur to Sir Bedivere:
" The sequel of to-day unsolders all
The goodliest fellowship of famous knights
Whereof this world holds record.   Such a sleep
They sleep—the men I loved.   I think that we
Shall never more, at any future time,

Delight our souls with talk of knightly deeds,
Walking about the gardens and the halls
Of Camelot, as in the days that were.
I perish by this people which I made,—
Though Merlin sware that I should come again
To rule once more—but let what will be, be,
I am so deeply smitten through the helm
That without help I cannot last till morn.
Thou therefore take my brand Excalibur,
Which was my pride: for thou rememberest how
In those old days, one summer noon, an arm
Rose up from out the bosom of the lake,
Clothed in white samite, mystic, wonderful,
Holding the sword—and how I rowed across
And took it, and have worn it, like a king:
And, wheresoever I am sung or told
In after time this also shall be known:
But now delay not: take Excalibur,
And fling him far into the middle mere:
Watch what thou seest, and lightly bring me word."

   To him replied the bold Sir Bedivere:
" It is not meet, Sir King, to leave thee thus,
Aidless, alone, and smitten through the helm.
A little thing may harm a wounded man.
Yet I thy hest will all perform at full,
Watch what I see, and lightly bring thee word."

   So saying, from the ruined shrine he stepped,
And in the moon athwart the place of tombs,

  7 *

Where lay the mighty bones of ancient men,
Old knights, and over them the sea-wind sang
Shrill, chill, with flakes of foam. He, stepping down
By zigzag paths, and juts of pointed rock,
Came on the shining levels of the lake.

There drew he forth the brand Excalibur,
And o'er him, drawing it, the winter moon,
Brightening the skirts of a long cloud, ran forth
And sparkled keen with frost against the hilt:
For all the haft twinkled with diamond sparks,
Myriads of topaz-lights, and jacinth-work
Of subtlest jewellery. He gazed so long
That both his eyes were dazzled, as he stood
This way and that dividing the swift mind,
In act to throw; but at the last it seemed
Better to leave Excalibur concealed
There in the many-knotted waterflags,
That whistled stiff and dry about the marge.
So strode he back slow to the wounded King.

Then spake King Arthur to Sir Bedivere:
"Hast thou performed my mission which I gave?
What is it thou hast seen? or what hast heard?"

And answer made the bold Sir Bedivere:
"I heard the ripple washing in the reeds,
And the wild water lapping on the crag."

To whom replied King Arthur, faint and pale:
"Thou hast betrayed thy nature and thy name,
Not rendering true answer, as beseemed

Thy fealty, nor like a noble knight :
For surer sign had followed, either hand
Or voice, or else a motion of the mere.
This is a shameful thing for men to lie.
Yet now, I charge thee, quickly go again
As thou art lief and dear, and do the thing
I bade thee, watch, and lightly bring me word."

    Then went Sir Bedivere the second time
Across the ridge, and paced beside the mere,
Counting the dewy pebbles, fixed in thought;
But when he saw the wonder of the hilt,
How curiously and strangely chased, he smote
His palms together, and he cried aloud.

    " And if indeed I cast the brand away,
Surely a precious thing, one worthy note,
Should thus be lost for ever from the earth,
Which might have pleased the eyes of many men.
What good should follow this, if this were done ?
What harm, undone ? deep harm to disobey,
Seeing obedience is the bond of rule.
Were it well to obey then, if a king demand
An act unprofitable, against himself ?
The king is sick, and knows not what he does.
What record, or what relic of my lord
Should be to aftertime, but empty breath
And rumors of a doubt ? but were this kept,
Stored in some treasure-house of mighty kings,
Some one might show it at a joust of arms,

Saying, " King Arthur's sword, Excalibur,
Wrought by the lonely maiden of the Lake.
Nine years she wrought it, sitting in the deeps
Upon the hidden bases of the hills."
So might some old man speak in the aftertime
To all the people, winning reverence.
But now much honor and much fame were lost."
  So spake he, clouded with his own conceit,
And hid Excalibur the second time,
And so strode back slow to the wounded King.
  Then spoke King Arthur, breathing heavily :
" What is it thou hast seen? or what hast heard?"
  And answer made the bold Sir Bedivere :
" I heard the water lapping on the crag,
And the long ripple washing in the reeds."
  To whom replied King Arthur, much in wrath :
" Ah, miserable and unkind, untrue,
Unknightly, traitor-hearted ! Woe is me !
Authority forgets a dying king,
Laid widowed of the power in his eye
That bowed the will. I see thee what thou art.
For thou, the latest left of all my knights,
In whom should meet the offices of all,
Thou wouldst betray me for the precious hilt ;
Either from lust of gold, or like a girl
Valuing the giddy pleasure of the eyes.
Yet, for a man may fail in duty twice,
And the third time may prosper, get thee hence :

But, if thou spare to fling Excalibur,
I will arise and slay thee with my hands."
    Then quickly rose Sir Bedivere, and ran,
And, leaping down the ridges lightly, plunged
Among the bulrush-beds, and clutched the sword,
And strongly wheeled and threw it. The great brand
Made lightnings in the splendor of the moon,
And flashing round and round, and whirled in an arch,
Shot like a streamer of the northern morn,
Seen where the moving isles of winter shock
By night, with noises of the northern sea.
So flashed and fell the brand Excalibur :
But ere he dipped the surface, rose an arm
Clothed in white samite, mystic, wonderful,
And caught him by the hilt, and brandished him
Three times, and drew him under in the meer.
And lightly went the other to the King.
    Then spoke King Arthur, drawing thicker breath?"
" Now see I by thine eyes that this is done.
Speak out : what is it thou hast heard, or seen
    And answer made the bold Sir Bedivere :
" Sir King, I closed mine eyelids, lest the gems
Should blind my purpose, for I never saw,
Nor shall see, here or elsewhere, till I die,
Not though I live three lives of mortal men,
So great a miracle as yonder hilt.
Then with both hands I flung him, wheeling him ;
But when I looked again, behold an arm,
Clothed in white samite, mystic, wonderful,

That caught him by the hilt, and brandished him
Three times, and drew him under in the mere."
    And answer made King Arthur, breathing hard :
" My end draws nigh ; 'tis time that I were gone.
Make broad thy shoulders to receive my weight
And bear me to the margin ; yet I fear
My wound hath taken cold, and I shall die."
    So saying, from the pavement he half rose,
Slowly, with pain, reclining on his arm,
And looking wistfully with wide blue eyes
As in a picture.   Him Sir Bedivere
Remorsefully regarded through his tears,
And would have spoken, but he found not words,
Then took with care, and kneeling on one knee,
O'er both his shoulders drew the languid hands,
And rising bore him through the place of tombs.
    But, as he walked, King Arthur panted hard,
Like one that feels a nightmare on his bed
When all the house is mute.   So sighed the King,
Muttering and murmuring at his ear, " Quick, quick !
I fear it is too late, and I shall die."
But the other swiftly strode from ridge to ridge,
Clothed with his breath, and looking, as he walked,
Larger than human on the frozen hills.
He heard the deep behind him, and a cry
Before.   His own thought drove him like a goad,
Dry clashed his harness in the icy caves
And barren chasms, and all to left and right

The bare black cliff clanged round him, as he based
His feet on juts of slippery crag that rang
Sharp-smitten with the dint of armed heels—
And on a sudden, lo! the level lake,
And the long glories of the winter moon.

Then saw they how there hove a dusky barge,
Dark as a funeral scarf from stem to stern,
Beneath them; and descending they were ware
That all the decks were dense with stately forms
Black-stoled, black-hooded, like a dream—by these
Three Queens with crowns of gold—and from them rose
A cry that shivered to the tingling stars,
And, as it were one voice, an agony
Of lamentation, like a wind, that shrills
All night in a waste land, where no one comes,
Or hath come, since the making of the world.
Then murmured Arthur, " Place me in the barge,
And to the barge they came.   There those three Queens
Put forth their hands, and took the King, and wept.
But she that rose the tallest of them all
And fairest, laid his head upon her lap,
And loosed the shattered casque, and chafed his hands,
And called him by his name, complaining loud,
And dropping bitter tears against his brow
Striped with dark blood: for all his face was white
And colorless, and like the withered moon
Smote by the fresh beam of the springing east;
And all his greaves and cuisses dashed with drops

Of onset: and the light and lustrous curls—
That made his forehead like a rising sun
High from the däis-throne—were parched with dust;
Or, clotted into points and hanging loose,
Mixed with the knightly growth that fringed his lips.
So like a shattered column lay the King;
Not like that Arthur who, with lance in rest,
From spur to plume a star of tournament,
Shot through the lists at Camelot, and charged
Before the eyes of ladies and of kings.

　　Then loudly cried the bold Sir Bedivere,
" Ah! my Lord Arthur, whither shall I go?
Where shall I hide my forehead and my eyes?
For now I see the true old times are dead,
When every morning brought a noble chance,
And every chance brought out a noble knight.
Such times have been not since the light that led
The holy Elders with the gift of myrrh.
But now the whole ROUND TABLE is dissolved
Which was an image of the mighty world;
And I, the last, go forth companionless.
And the days darken round me, and the years,
Among new men, strange faces, other minds."

　　And slowly answered Arthur from the barge:
" The old order changeth, yielding place to new,
And God fulfils himself in many ways,
Lest one good custom should corrupt the world.
Comfort thyself: what comfort is in me?

I have lived my life, and that which I have done
May He within himself make pure! but thou,
If thou shouldst never see my face again,
Pray for my soul. More things are wrought by prayer
Than this world dreams of. Wherefore, let thy voice
Rise like a fountain for me night and day.
For what are men better than sheep or goats
That nourish a blind life within the brain, .
If, knowing God, they lift not hands of prayer
Both for themselves and those who call them friend?
For so the whole round earth is every way
Bound by gold chains about the feet of God.
But now farewell. I am going a long way
With these thou seest—if indeed I go
(For all my mind is clouded with a doubt)
To the island-valley of Avilion;
Where falls not hail, or rain, or any snow,
Nor ever wind blows loudly; but it lies
Deep-meadowed, happy, fair with orchard-lawns
And bowery hollows crowned with summer sea,
Where I will heal me of my grievous wound."

So said he, and the barge with oar and sail
Moved from the brink, like some full-breasted swan,
That, fluting a wild carol, ere her death,
Ruffles her pure cold plume, and takes the flood
With swarthy webs. Long stood Sir Bedivere
Revolving many memories, till the hull
Looked one black dot against the verge of dawn,
And on the meer the wailing died away.

THE SEA-FAIRIES.

SLOW sailed the weary mariners, and saw,
Betwixt the green brink and the running foam,
Sweet faces, rounded arms, and bosoms pressed
To little harps of gold; and, while they mused,
Whispering to each other half in fear,
Shrill music reached them on the middle sea.

Whither away, whither away, whither away? fly no more.
Whither away from the high green field, and the happy blossom-
    ing shore?
Day and night to the billow the fountain calls;
Down shower the gambolling waterfalls
From wandering over the lea:
Out of the live-green heart of the dells
They freshen the silvery-crimson shells,
And thick with white bells the clover-hill swells
High over the full-toned sea:
O hither, come hither, and furl your sails,
Come hither to me and to me!
Hither, come hither, and frolic and play;
Here it is only the mew that wails;
We will sing to you all the day:
Mariner, mariner, furl your sails,
For here are the blissful downs and dales,
And merrily, merrily carol the gales,
And the spangle dances in bight and bay,

And the rainbow forms and flies on the land
Over the islands free;
And the rainbow lives in the curve of the sand;
Hither, come hither and see;
And the rainbow hangs on the poising wave,
And sweet is the color of cove and cave,
And sweet shall your welcome be;
O hither, come hither, and be our lords,
For merry brides are we!
We will kiss sweet kisses, and speak sweet words:
O listen, listen, your eyes shall glisten
With pleasure and love and jubilee!
O listen, listen, your eyes shall glisten
When the sharp, clear twang of the golden chords
Runs up the ridgèd sea!
Who can light on as happy a shore
All the world o'er, all the world o'er?
Whither away? listen and stay: mariner, mariner, fly no more.

GODIVA.

I waited for the train at Coventry;
I hung with grooms and porters on the bridge,
To watch the three tall spires; and there I shaped
The city's ancient legend into this:—

Not only we, the latest seed of Time,
New men, that in the flying of a wheel

Cry down the past, not only we, that prate
Of rights and wrongs, have loved the people well,
And loathed to see them overtaxed; but she
Did more, and underwent, and overcame,
The woman of a thousand summers back,
Godiva, wife of that grim Earl, who ruled
In Coventry : for when he laid a tax
Upon his town, and all the mothers brought
Their children, clamoring, "If we pay, we starve!
She sought her lord, and found him, where he strode
About the hall, among his dogs, alone,
His beard a foot before him, and his hair
A yard behind   She told him of their tears,
And prayed him, " If they pay this tax, they starve '
Whereat he stared, replying half amazed,
" You would not let your little finger ache
For such as this?"—" But I would die," said she
He laughed, and swore by Peter and by Paul:
Then fillipped at the diamond in her ear;
" O ay, ay, ay, you talk !" — " Alas !" she said,
" But prove me what it is I would not do."
And from a heart as rough as Esau's hand,
He answered, " Ride you naked through the town,
And I repeal it ;" and nodding, as in scorn,
He parted, with great strides among his dogs

   So left alone, the passions of her mind,
As winds from all the compass shift and blow,
Made war upon each other for an hour,

Till pity won. She sent a herald forth,
And bade him cry, with sound of trumpet, all
The hard condition ; but that she would loose
The people : therefore, as they loved her well,
From then till noon no foot should pace the street,
No eye look down, she passing ; but that all
Should keep within, door shut, and window barred.

Then fled she to her inmost bower, and there
Unclasped the wedded eagles of her belt,
The grim Earl's gift ; but ever at a breath
She lingered, looking like a summer moon
Half-dipped in cloud : anon she shook her head,
And showered the rippled ringlets to her knee,
Unclad herself in haste ; adown the stair
Stole on ; and, like a creeping sunbeam, slid
From pillar unto pillar, until she reached
The gateway ; there she found her palfrey trapped
In purple blazoned with armorial gold.

Then she rode forth, clothed on with chastity :
The deep air listened round her as she rode,
And all the low wind hardly breathed for fear.
The little wide-mouthed heads upon the spout
Had cunning eyes to see : the barking cur
Made her cheek flame : her palfrey's footfall shot
Light horrors through her pulses : the blind walls
Were full of chinks and holes ; and overhead
Fantastic gables, crowding, stared : but she
Not less through all bore up, till, last, she saw
   8 *

The whit: flowered elder thicket from the field
Gleam through the Gothic archways in the wall.
  Then she rode back, clothed on with chastity.
And one low churl, compact of thankless earth,
The fatal byword of all years to come,
Boring a little auger-hole in fear,
Peeped—but his eyes, before they had their will,
Were shrivelled into darkness in his head,
And dropped before him. So the Powers, who wait
On noble deeds, cancelled a sense misused;
And she, that knew not, passed: and all at once,
With twelve great shocks of sound, the shameless noon
Was clashed and hammered from a hundred towers,
One after one: but even then she gained
Her bower; whence reissuing, robed and crowned,
To meet her lord, she took the tax away,
And built herself an everlasting name.

SIR GALAHAD.

My good blade carves the casques of men,
  My tough lance thrusteth sure,
My strength is as the strength of ten,
  Because my heart is pure.
The shattering trumpet shrilleth high,
  The hard brands shiver on the steel,
The splintered spear-shafts crack and fly,
  The horse and rider reel:

They reel, they roll in clanging lists,
   And when the tide of combat stands,
Perfume and flowers fall in showers,
   That lightly rain from ladie's hands.

How sweet are looks that ladies bend
   On whom their favors fall !
For them I battle till the end,
   To save from shame and thrall:
But all my heart is drawn above,
   My knees are bowed in crypt and shrine :
I never felt the kiss of love,
   Nor maiden's hand in mine.
More bounteous aspects on me beam,
   Me mightier transports move and thrill;
So keep I fair through faith and prayer
   A virgin heart in work and will.

When down the the stormy crescent goes,
   A light before me swims,
Between dark stems the forest glows,
   I hear a noise of hymns :
Then by some secret shrine I ride ;
   I hear a voice, but none are there ;
The stalls are void, the doors are wide,
   The tapers burning fair.
Fair gleams the snowy altar-cloth,
   The silver vessels sparkle clean.
The shrill bell rings, the censer swings,
   And solemn chants resound between.

Sometimes on lonely mountain-meres
  I find a magic bark ;
I leap on board : no helmsman steers :
  I float till all is dark.
A gentle sound, an awful light !
  Three angels bear the holy Grail :
With folded feet, in stoles of white,
  On sleeping wings they sail.
Ah, blessed vision ! blood of God !
  My spirit beats her mortal bars,
As down dark tides the glory slides,
  And star-light mingles with the stars.

When on my goodly charger borne
  Through dreaming towns I go,
The cock crows ere the Christmas morn,
  The streets are dumb with snow.
The tempest crackles on the leads,
  And, ringing, spins from brand and mail·
But o'er the dark a glory spreads,
  And gilds the driving hail.
I leave the plain, I climb the height ;
  No branchy thicket shelter yields ;
But blessed forms in whistling storms
  Fly o'er waste fens and windy fields.

A maiden knight—to me is given
  Such hope, I know not fear ;
I yearn to breathe the airs of heaven
  That often meet me here.

I muse on joy that will not cease,
  Pure spaces clothed in living beams,
Pure lilies of eternal peace,
  Whose odors haunt my dreams;
And, stricken by an angel's hand,
  This mortal armor that I wear,
This weight and size, this heart and eyes,
  Are touched, are turned to finest air.

The clouds are broken in the sky,
  And through the mountain-walls
A rolling organ-harmony
  Swells up, and shakes and falls.
Then move the trees, the copses nod,
  Wings flutter, voices hover clear:
"O just and faithful knight of God!
  Ride on! the prize is near."
So pass I hostel, hall, and grange;
  By bridge and ford, by park and pale,
All-armed I ride, whate'er betide,
  Until I find the holy Grail.

THE LORD OF BURLEIGH.

In her ear he whispers gayly,
  "If my heart by signs can tell,
Maiden, I have watched thee daily,
  And I think thou lov'st me well."

She replies, in accents fainter,
  "There is none I love like thee."
He is but a landscape-painter,
  And a village maiden she.
He to lips, that fondly falter,
  Presses his without reproof;
Leads her to the village altar,
  And they leave her father's roof.
" I can make no marriage present;
  Little can I give my wife.
Love will make our cottage pleasant,
  And I love thee more than life."
They by parks and lodges going
  See the lordly castles stand :
Summer woods, about them blowing,
  Made a murmur in the land.
From deep thought himself he rouses,
  Says to her that loves him well,
" Let us see these handsome houses
  Where the wealthy nobles dwell."
So she goes by him attended,
  Hears him lovingly converse,
Sees whatever fair and splendid
  Lay betwixt his home and hers;
Parks with oak and chestnut shady,
  Parks and ordered gardens great,
Ancient homes of lord and lady,
  Built for pleasure and for state.

All he shows her makes him dearer :
    Evermore she seems to gaze
On that cottage growing nearer,
    Where they twain will spend their days.
O but she will love him truly !
    He shall have a cheerful home ;
She will order all things duly,
    When beneath his roof they come.
Thus her heart rejoices greatly,
    Till a gateway she discerns
With armorial bearings stately,
    And beneath the gate she turns ;
Sees a mansion more majestic
    Than all those she saw before ;
Many a gallant gay domestic
    Bows before him at the door.
And they speak in gentle murmur,
    When they answer to his call,
While he treads with footstep firmer,
    Leading on from hall to hall.
And, while now she wonders blindly,
    Nor the meaning can divine,
Proudly turns he round and kindly,
    " All of this is mine and thine."
Here he lives in state and bounty,
    Lord of Burleigh, fair and free,
Not a lord in all the county
    Is so great a lord as he.

All at once the color flushes
  Her sweet face from brow to chin :
As it were with shame she blushes,
  And her spirit changed within.
Then her countenance all over
  Pale again as death did prove :
But he clasped her like a lover,
  And he cheered her soul with love.
So she strove against her weakness,
  Though at times her spirit sank :
Shaped her heart with woman's meekness
  To all duties of her rank :
And a gentle consort made he,
  And her gentle mind was such
That she grew a noble lady,
  And the people loved her much.
But a trouble weighed upon her,
  And perplexed her, night and morn,
With the burthen of an honor
  Unto which she was not born.
Faint she grew, and ever fainter,
  As she murmured, " O, that he
Were once more that landscape-painter
  Which did win my heart from me !"
So she drooped and drooped before him,
  Fading slowly from his side :
Three fair children first she bore him,
  Then before her time she died.

Weeping, weeping late and early,
   Walking up and pacing down,
Deeply mourned the Lord of Burleigh,
   Burleigh-house by Stamford town.
And he came to look upon her,
   And he looked at her and said,
" Bring the dress, and put it on her
   That she wore when she was wed."
Then her people, softly treading,
   Bore to earth her body, dressed
In the dress that she was wed in,
   That her spirit might have rest.

"AS THROUGH THE LAND."

As through the land at eve we went,
   And plucked the ripened ears,
We fell out, my wife and I,
O, we fell out, I know not why,
   And kissed again with tears.

For when we came where lies the child
   We lost in other years,
There above the little grave,
O, there above the little grave,
   We kissed again with tears.

SWEET AND LOW.

SWEET and low, sweet and low,
  Wind of the western sea,
Low, low, breathe and blow,
  Wind of the western sea!
Over the rolling waters go,
Come from the dying moon, and blow,
  Blow him again to me;
While my little one, while my pretty one, sleeps.

Sleep and rest, sleep and rest,
  Father will come to thee soon;
Rest, rest, on mother's breast,
  Father will come to thee soon;
Father will come to his babe in the nest,
Silver sails all out of the west,
  Under the silver moon;
Sleep, my little one, sleep, my pretty one, sleep.

HOME THEY BROUGHT HER WARRIOR DEAD

HOME they brought her warrior dead:
  She nor swooned, nor uttered cry:
All her maidens, watching, said,
  "She must weep or she will die."

Then they praised him, soft and low,
    Called him worthy to be loved,
Truest friend and noblest foe;
    Yet she neither spoke nor moved.

Stole a maiden from her place,
    Lightly to the warrior stepped,
Took the face-cloth from the face:
    Yet she neither moved nor wept.

Rose a nurse of ninety years,
    Set his child upon her knee—
Like summer tempest came her tears—
    " Sweet my child, I live for thee."

THE BUGLE SONG.

The splendor falls on castle walls
    And snowy summits old in story;
The long light shakes across the lakes,
    And the wild cataract leaps in glory.
Blow, bugle, blow, set the wild echoes flying.
Blow, bugle; answer, echoes, dying, dying, dying.

O hark, O hear! how thin and clear,
    And thinner, clearer, farther going;
O sweet and far, from cliff and scar,
    The horns of Elfland faintly blowing!
Blow, let us hear the purple glens replying:
Blow, bugle; answer, echoes, dying, dying, dying.

O love, they die in yon rich sky,
   They faint on hill or field or river:
Our echoes roll from soul to soul,
   And grow for ever and for ever.
Blow, bugle, blow, set the wild echoes flying,
And answer, echoes, answer, dying, dying, dying.

•

"ASK ME NO MORE."

Ask me no more: the moon may draw the sea;
  The cloud may stoop from heaven and take the shape
  With fold to fold, of mountain or of cape;
But, O too fond, when have I answered thee?
     Ask me no more.

Ask me no more: what answer should I give?
  I love not hollow cheek or faded eye:
  Yet, O my friend, I will not have thee die!
Ask me no more, lest I should bid thee live!
     Ask me no more.

Ask me no more: thy fate and mine are sealed:
  I strove against the stream and all in vain:
  Let the great river take me to the main:
No more, dear love, for at a touch I yield;
     Ask me no more.

WHAT DOES LITTLE BIRDIE SAY.

WHAT does little birdie say
In her nest at peep of day?
Let me fly, says little birdie,
Mother, let me fly away.
Birdie, rest a little longer,
Till the little wings are stronger.
So she rests a little longer
Then she flies away.

What does little baby say,
In her bed at peep of day?
Baby says, like little birdie,
Let me rise and fly away.
Baby, sleep a little longer,
Till the little limbs are stronger
If she sleeps a little longer
Baby too shall fly away.

TO THE QUEEN.

FROM " THE IDYLLS OF THE KING."

THESE to his memory—since he led them dear, .
Perchance as finding there unconsciously
Some image of himself—I dedicate,
I dedicate, I consecrate with tears—
These Idylls.

9 *

And indeed he seems to me
Scarce other than my own ideal knight,
" Who reverenced his conscience as his king ;
Whose glory was, redressing human wrong ;
Who spake no slander, no, nor listened to it ;
Who loved one only and who clave to her "—
Her—over all whose realms to their last isle,
Commingled with the gloom of imminent war
The shadow of his loss moved like eclipse,
Darkening the world.   We have lost him : he is gone
We know him now : all narrow jealousies
Are silent ; and we see him as he moved,
How modest, kindly, all accomplished, wise,
With what sublime repression of himself,
And in what limits, and how tenderly ;
Not swaying to this faction or to that ;
Not making his high place the lawless perch
Of winged ambitions, nor a vantage ground
For pleasure ; but through all this tract of years
Wearing the white flower of a blameless life,
Before a thousand peering littlenesses,
In that fierce light which beats upon a throne,
And blackens every blot : for where is he,
Who dare foreshadow for an only son
A lovelier life, a more unstained, than his ?
Or how should England dreaming of *his* sons
Hope more for these than some inheritance
Of such a life, a heart a mind as thine.

Thou noble Father of her Kings to be,
Laborious for her people and her poor—
Voice in the rich dawn of an ampler day—
Far-sighted summoner of war and waste
To fruitful strifes and rivalries of peace—
Sweet nature gilded by the gracious gleam
Of letters, dear to Science, dear to Art,
Dear to thy land and ours, a Prince indeed,
Beyond all titles, and a household name,
Hereafter, through all times, Albert the Good.

  Break not, O woman's heart, but still endure ;
Break not, for thou art Royal, but endure,
Remembering all the beauty of that star
Which shone so close beside thee, that ye made
One light together, but has past and left
The Crown a lonely splendor.

             May all love,
His love, unseen but felt, o'ershadow thee,
The love of all thy sons encompass thee,
The love of all thy daughters cherish thee,
The love of all thy people comfort thee,
Till God's love set thee at his side again !

LOCKSLEY HALL.

COMRADES, leave me here a little, while as yet 'tis early morn:
Leave me here, and when you want me, sound upon the bugle-
 horn.

'Tis the place, and all around it, as of old, the curlews call.
Dreary gleams about the moorland flying over Locksley Hall;

Locksley Hall, that in the distance overlooks the sandy tracts,
And the hollow ocean-ridges roaring into cataracts.

Many a night from yonder ivied casement, ere I went to rest,
Did I look on great Orion sloping slowly to the West.

Many a night I saw the Pleiads, rising through the mellow shade,
Glitter like a swarm of fire-flies tangled in a silver braid.

Here about the beach I wandered, nourishing a youth sublime
With the fairy tales of science, and the long result of Time;

When the centuries behind me like a fruitful land reposed;
When I clung to all the present for the promise that it closed:

When I dipped into the future far as human eye could see;
Saw the Vision of the world, and all the wonder that would be.—

In the Spring a fuller crimson comes upon the Robin's breast;
In the Spring the wanton lapwing gets himself another crest;

In the Spring a livelier iris changes on the burnished dove;
In the Spring a young man's fancy lightly turns to thoughts of
  love.

Then her cheek was pale and thinner than should be for one so
  young,
And her eyes on all my motions with a mute observance hung.

And I said, "My cousin Amy, speak, and speak the truth to me,
Trust me, cousin, all the current of my being sets to thee."

On her pallid cheek and forehead came a color and a light,
As I have seen the rosy red flushing in the northern night.

And she turned—her bosom shaken with a sudden storm of
  sighs—
All the spirit deeply dawning in the dark of hazel eyes—

Saying, "I have hid my feelings, fearing they should do me
  wrong;"
Saying, "Dost thou love me, cousin?" weeping, "I have loved
  thee long."

Love took up the glass of Time, and turned it in his glowing
  hands;
Every moment, lightly shaken, ran itself in golden sands.

Love took up the harp of Life, and smote on all the chords with
  might;
Smote the chord of Self, that, trembling, passed in music out of
  sight.

Many a morning on the moorland did we hear the copses ring,
And her whisper thronged my pulses with the fulness of the
    Spring.

Many an evening by the waters did we watch the stately ships,
And our spirits rushed together at the touching of the lips.

O my cousin, shallow-hearted!   O my Amy, mine no more!
O the dreary, dreary moorland!   O the barren, barren shore!

Falser than all fancy fathoms, falser than all songs have sung,
Puppet to a father's threat, and servile to a shrewish tongue!

Is it well to wish thee happy?—having known me—to decline
On a range of lower feelings and a narrower heart than mine!

Yet it shall be : thou shalt lower to his level day by day,
What is fine within thee growing coarse to sympathize with clay.

As the husband is, the wife is; thou art mated with a clown,
And the grossness of his nature will have weight to drag thee
    down.

He will hold thee, when his passion shall have spent its novel
    force,
Something better than his dog, a little dearer than his horse.

What is this? his eyes are heavy : think not they are glazed with
    wine.
Go to him : it is thy duty : kiss him : take his hand in thine.

It may be my lord is weary, that his brain is over wrought :
Soothe him with thy finer fancies, touch him with thy lighter
thought.

He will answer to the purpose, easy things to understand—
Better thou wert dead before me, though I slew thee with my
hand !

Better thou and I were lying, hidden from the heart's disgrace,
Rolled in one another's arms, and silent in a last embrace.

Cursed be the social wants that sin against the strength of youth !
Cursed be the social lies that warp us from the living truth !

Cursed be the sickly forms that err from honest Nature's rule !
Cursed be the gold that gilds the straitened forehead of the fool !

Well,—'tis well that I should bluster !—Hadst thou less unworthy
proved—
Would to God—for I had loved thee more than ever wife was
loved.

Am I mad, that I should cherish that which bears but bitter fruit ?
I will pluck it from my bosom, though my heart be at the root.

Never, though my mortal summers to such length of years should
come
As the many-wintered crow that leads the clanging rookery-home.

Where is comfort ? in division of the records of the mind ?
Can I part her from herself and love her, as I knew her, kind ?

I remember one that perished : sweetly did she speak and move :
Such a one do I remember, whom to look at was to love.

Can I think of her as dead, and love her for the love she bore ?
No—she never loved me truly : love is love for evermore.

Comfort? comfort scorned of devils ! this is truth the poet sings,
That a sorrow's crown of sorrow is remembering happier things.

Drug thy memories, lest thou learn it, lest thy heart be put to
    proof,
In the dead, unhappy night, and when the rain is on the roof.

Like a dog, he hunts in dreams, and thou art staring at the wall,
Where the dying night-lamp flickers, and the shadows rise and
    fall.

Then a hand would pass before thee, pointing to his drunken sleep,
To thy widowed marriage-pillows, to the tears that thou wilt weep.

Thou shalt hear the " Never, never," whispered by the phantom
    years,
And a song from out the distance in the ringing of thine ears.

And an eye shall vex thee, looking ancient kindness on thy pain.
Turn thee, turn thee on thy pillow ; get thee to thy rest again.

Nay, but Nature brings thee solace ; for a tender voice will cry.
'Tis a purer life than thine ; a lip to drain thy trouble dry.

Baby lips will laugh me down : my latest rival brings thee rest.
Baby fingers, waxen touches, press me from the mother's breast

O, the child too clothes the father with a dearness not his due.
Half is thine and half is his : it will be worthy of the two.

O, I see thee old and formal, fitted to thy petty part,
With a little hoard of maxims preaching down a daughter's heart

"They were dangerous guides the feelings—she herself was not
    exempt—
Truly, she herself had suffered"—Perish in thy self-contempt !

Overlive it—lower yet—be happy ! wherefore should I care ?
I myself must mix with action, lest I wither by despair.

What is that which I should turn to, lighting upon days like
    these ?
Every door is barred with gold, and opens but to golden keys.

Every gate is thronged with suitors, all the markets overflow.
I have but an angry fancy : what is that which I should do?

I had been content to perish, falling on the foeman's ground,
When the ranks are rolled in vapor, and the winds are laid with
    sound.

But the jingling of the guinea helps the hurt that Honor feels,
And the nations do but murmur, snarling at each other's heels.

Can I but relive in sadness? I will turn that earlier page.
Hide me from my deep emotion, oh thou wondrous Mother-Age !

Make me feel the wild pulsation that I felt before the strife,
When I heard my days before me, and the tumult of my life ;
    10 .

Yearning for the large excitement that the coming years would
    yield,
Eager-hearted as a boy when first he leaves his father's field,

And at night along the dusky highway near and nearer drawn,
Sees in heaven the light of London flaring like a dreary dawn;

And his spirit leaps within him to be gone before him then,
Underneath the light he looks at, in among the throngs of men;

Men, my brothers, men the workers, ever reaping something new :
That which they have done but earnest of the things that they
    shall do :

For I dipped into the future, far as human eye could see,
Saw the Vision of the world, and all the wonder that would be ;

Saw the heavens fill with commerce, argosies of magic sails,
Pilots of the purple twilight, dropping down with costly bales ;

Heard the heavens fill with shouting, and there rained a ghastly
    dew
From the nations' airy navies grappling in the central blue ;

Far along the world-wide whisper of the south-wind rushing warm,
With the standards of the peoples plunging through the thunder-
    storm ;

Till the war-drum throbbed no longer, and the battle-flags were
    furled
In the Parliament of man, the Federation of the world ;

There the common sense of most shall hold a fretful realm in awe,
And the kindly earth shall slumber, lapped in universal law.

So I triumphed, ere my passion sweeping through me left me dry,
Left me with the palsied heart, and left me with the jaundiced
eye;

Eye, to which all order festers, all things here are out of joint,
Science moves, but slowly, slowly, creeping on from point to point:

Slowly comes a hungry people, as a lion, creeping nigher,
Glares at one that nods and winks behind a slowly-dying fire.

Yet I doubt not through the ages one increasing purpose runs,
And the thoughts of men are widened with the process of the
suns.

What is that to him that reaps not harvest of his youthful joys,
Though the deep heart of existence beat for ever like a boy's?

Knowledge comes, but wisdom lingers, and I linger on the shore,
And the individual withers, and the world is more and more.

Knowledge comes, but wisdom lingers, and he bears a laden
breast,
Full of sad experience moving toward the stillness of his rest.

Hark, my merry comrades call me, sounding on the bugle-horn,
They to whom my foolish passion were a target for their scorn:

Shall it not be scorn to me to harp on such a mouldered string?
I am shamed through all my nature to have loved so slight a thing.

Weakness to be wroth with weakness! woman's pleasure, woman's
    pain—
Nature made them blinder motions bounded in a shallower brain:

Woman is the lesser man, and all thy passions, matched with
    mine,
Are as moonlight unto sunlight, and as water unto wine—

Here at least, where nature sickens, nothing.   Ah, for some re-
    treat
Deep in yonder shining Orient, where my life began to beat;

Where in wild Mahratta-battle fell my father evil-starred;
I was left a trampled orphan, and a selfish uncle's ward.

Or to burst all links of habit—there to wander far away,
On from island unto island at the gateways of the day.

Larger constellations burning, mellow moons and happy skies,
Breadths of tropic shade and palms in cluster, knots of Paradise.

Never comes the trader, never floats an European flag,
Slides the bird o'er lustrous woodland, swings the trailer from the
    crag;

Droops the heavy-blossomed bower, hangs the heavy-fruited tree;
Summer isles of Eden lying in dark-purple spheres of sea.

There methinks would be enjoyment more than in this march of
    mind,
In the steamship, in the railway, in the thoughts that shake man-
    kind.

There the passions, cramped no longer, shall have scope and
    breathing-space ;
I will take some savage woman, she shall rear my dusky race.

Iron-jointed, supple-sinewed, they shall dive, and they shall run,
Catch the wild goat by the hair, and hurl their lances in the sun ;

Whistle back the parrot's call, and leap the rainbows of the brooks,
Not with blinded eyesight poring over miserable books—

Fool, again the dream, the fancy ! but I *know* my words are wild,
But I count the gray barbarian lower than the Christian child.

I, to herd with narrow foreheads, vacant of our glorious gains,
Like a beast with lower pleasures, like a beast with lower pains !

Mated with a squalid savage—what to me were sun or clime ?
I the heir of all the ages, in the foremost files of time—

I that rather held it better men should perish one by one,
Than that earth should stand at gaze like Joshua's moon in
    Ajalon !

Not in vain the distance beacons. Forward, forward let us range.
Let the great world spin for ever down the ringing grooves of
    change

Through the shadow of the globe we sweep into the younger day :
Better fifty years of Europe than a cycle of Cathay.   •
   10*

Mother-age, (for mine I knew not,) help me as when life begun :
Rift the hills, and roll the waters, flash the lightnings, weigh the
    Sun—

O, I see the crescent promise of my spirit hath not set.
Ancient founts of inspiration well through all my fancy yet.

Howsoever these things be, a long farewell to Locksley Hall !
Now for me the woods may wither, now for me the roof-tree fall.

Comes a vapor from the margin, blackening over heath and holt,
Cramming all the blast before it, in its breast a thunderbolt.

Let it fall on Locksley Hall, with rain or hail, or fire or snow ;
For the mighty wind arises, roaring seaward, and I go.

THE ISLET.

"WHITHER, O whither, love, shall we go,
For a score of sweet little summers or so?"
The sweet little wife of the singer said,
On the day that followed the day she was wed,
"Whither O whither, love, shall we go?"
And the singer shaking his curly head
Turned as he sat, and struck the keys
There at his right with a sudden crash.
Singing, "and shall it be over the seas
With a crew that is neither rude nor rash,

But a bevy of Eroses apple-cheeked,
In a shallop of crystal ivory-beaked,
With a satin sail of a ruby glow,
To a sweet little Eden on earth that I know,
A mountain islet pointed and peaked;
Waves on a diamond shingle dash,
Cataract brooks to the ocean run,
Fairily-delicate palaces shine
Mixed with myrtle and clad with vine,
And overstreamed and silvery-streaked
With many a rivulet high against the Sun
The facets of the glorious mountain flash
Above the valleys of palm and pine."

"Thither, O thither, love, let us go."

" No, no, no!
For in all that exquisite isle, my dear,
There is but one bird with a musical throat,
And his compass is but of a single note,
That it makes one weary to hear."

" Mock me not! mock me not! love, let us go."

" No, love, no.
For the bud ever breaks into bloom on the tree,
And a storm never wakes on the lonely sea,
And a worm is there in the lonely wood,
That pierces the liver and blackens the blood,
And makes it a sorrow to be."

THE SLEEPING BEAUTY.

YEAR after year unto her feet,
  She lying on her couch alone,
Across the purple coverlet.
  The maiden's jet-black hair has grown,
  On either side her trancèd form
Forth streaming from a braid of pearl:
  The slumbrous light is rich and warm,
  And moves not on the rounded curl.

The silk star-broidered coverlid   -
  Unto her limbs itself doth mould
Languidly ever; and, amid
  Her full black ringlets downward rolled,
Glows forth each softly-shadowed arm
  With bracelets of the diamond bright:
  Her constant beauty doth inform
  Stillness with love, and day with light.

She sleeps: her breathings are not heard
  In palace chambers far apart.
The fragrant tresses are not stirred
  That lie upon her charmèd heart.
She sleeps: on either hand upswells
  The gold-fringed pillow lightly pressed:
She sleeps, nor dreams, but ever dwells
  A perfect form in perfect rest.

THE RINGLET.

" YOUR ringlets, your ringlets,
    That look so golden-gay,
If you will give me one, but one,
    To kiss it night and day,
Then never chilling touch of Time
    Will turn it silver-gray ;
And then shall I know it is all true gold
To flame and sparkle and stream as of old,
Till all the comets in heaven are cold,
    And all her stars decay."
" Then take it, love, and put it by ;
This cannot change, nor yet can I."

" My ringlet, my ringlet,
    That art so golden-gay,
Now never chilling touch of Time
    Can turn thee silver-gray ;
And a lad may wink, and a girl may hint,
    And a fool may say his say ;
For my doubts and fears were all amiss,
And I swear henceforth by this and this,
That a doubt will only come for a kiss,
    And a fear to be kissed away."
" Then kiss it, love, and put it by :
If this can change, why so can I."

O Ringlet, O Ringlet,
    I kissed you night and day,

And Ringlet, O Ringlet,
    You still are golden-gay,
But Ringlet, O Ringlet,
    You should be silver-gray :
For what is this which now I'm told,
I that took you for true gold,
She that gave you's bought and sold,
        Sold, sold.

O Ringlet, O Ringlet,
    She blushed a rosy red.
When Ringlet, O Ringlet,
    She clipped you from her head,
And Ringlet, O Ringlet,
    She gave you me, and said,
" Come, kiss it, love, and put it by :
    If this can change, why so can I."
O fie, you golden nothing, fie
        You golden lie.

O Ringlet, O Ringlet,
    I count you much to blame,
For Ringlet, O Ringlet,
    You put me much to shame,
So Ringlet, O Ringlet,
    I doom you to the flame.
For what is this which now I learn,
    Has given all my faith a turn ?
Burn, you glossy heretic, burn,
        Burn, burn.

A WELCOME TO ALEXANDRA.

MARCH 7, 1863.

SEA-KINGS' daughter from over the sea,
                              Alexandra !
Saxon and Norman and Dane are we,
But all of us Danes in our welcome of thee,
                              Alexandra !
Welcome her, thunders of fort and of fleet !
Welcome her, thundering cheer of the street !
Welcome her, all things youthful and sweet,
Scatter the blossom under her feet !
Break, happy land, into earlier flowers !
Make music, O bird, in the new-budded bowers !
Blazon your mottos of blessing and prayer !
Welcome her, welcome her, all that is ours !
Warble, O bugle, and trumpet, blare !
Flags, flutter out upon turrets and towers !
Flames, on the windy headland flare !
Utter your jubilee, steeple and spire !
Clash, ye bells, in the merry March air !
Flash, ye cities, in rivers of fire !
Rush to the roof, sudden rocket, and higher
Melt into stars for the land's desire !
Roll and rejoice, jubilant voice,
Roll as a ground-swell dashed on the strand,
Roar as the sea when he welcomes the land,
And welcome her, welcome the land's desire,

The sea-kings' daug' 'er as happy as fair,
Blissful bride of a blissful heir,
Bride of the heir of the kings of the sea—
O joy to the people and joy to the throne,
Come to us, love us, and make us your own:
For Saxon or Dane or Norman we,
Teuton or Celt, or whatever we be,
We are each all Dane in our welcome of thee,
                            Alexandra!

ODE

SUNG AT THE OPENING OF THE INTERNATIONAL EXHIBITION.

UPLIFT a thousand voices full and sweet,
    In this wide hall with earth's inventions stored,
    And praise the invisible universal Lord,
Who lets once more in peace the nations meet,
    Where Science, Art, and Labor have outpoured
Their myriad horns of plenty at our feet.

O silent father of our Kings to be
Mourned in this golden hour of jubilee,
For this, for all, we weep our thanks to thee!

        The world-compelling plan was thine,
        And, lo! the long laborious miles
        Of Palace; lo! the giant aisles,
        Rich in model and design;

Harvest-tool and husbandry,
Loom and wheel and enginery,
Secrets of the sullen mine,
Steel and gold, and corn and wine,
Fabric rough, or Fairy fine,
Sunny tokens of the Line,
Polar marvels, and a feast
Of wonder, out of West and East,
And shapes and hues of part divine!
All of beauty, all of use,
That one fair planet can produce.
Brought from under every star,
Blown from over every main,
And mixed, as life is mixed with pain,
The works of peace with works of war.

O ye, the wise who think, the wise who reign,
From growing commerce loose her latest chain,
And let the fair white-winged peacemaker fly
To happy havens under all the sky,
And mix the seasons and the golden hours,
Till each man finds his own in all men's good,
And all men work in noble brotherhood,
Breaking their mailèd fleets and armèd towers,
And ruling by obeying Nature's powers,
And gathering all the fruits of peace and crowned with all her
    flowers.

11

THE SAILOR-BOY.

HE rose at dawn and, fired with hope,
    Shot o'er the seething harbor-bar,
And reached the ship and caught the rope,
    And whistled to the morning star.

And while he whistled long and loud
    He heard a fierce mermaiden cry,
" O boy, though thou art young and proud,
    I see the place where thou wilt lie.

"The sands and yeasty surges mix
    In caves about the dreary bay,
And on thy ribs the limpet sticks,
    And in thy heart the scrawl shall play."

" Fool," he answered, " death is sure
    To those that stay and those that roam,
But I will nevermore endure
    To sit with empty hands at home.

" My mother clings about my neck,
    My sisters crying 'stay for shame ;'
My father raves of death and wreck,
    They are all to blame, they are all to blame.

" God help me! save I take my part
    Of danger on the roaring sea,
A devil rises in my heart,
    Far worse than any death to me."

IN THE VALLEY OF CAUTERETZ.

ALL along the valley, stream that flashest white
Deepening thy voice with the deepening of the night,
All along the valley, where thy waters flow,
I walked with one I loved two-and-thirty years ago.
All along the valley while I walked to-day,
The two-and-thirty years were a mist that rolls away;
For all along the valley, down thy rocky bed
Thy living voice to me was as the voice of the dead,
And all along the valley, by rock and cave and tree,
The voice of the dead was a living voice to me.

THE FLOWER.

ONCE in a golden hour
    I cast to earth a seed.
Up there came a flower,
    The people said, a weed.

To and fro they went
    Through my garden-bower,
And muttering discontent
    Cursed me and my flower.

Then it grew so tall
    It wore a crown of light,

But thieves from o'er the wall
    Stole the seed by night.

Sowed it far and wide
    By every town and tower,
Till all the people cried
    " Splendid is the flower."

Read my little fable :
    He that runs may read.
Most can raise the flowers now,
    For all have got the seed.

And some are pretty enough,
    And some are poor indeed ;
And now again the people
    Call it but a weed.

.

.

THE END.

.

PRINTED BY I. ASHMEAD.

www.ingramcontent.com/pod-product-compliance
Lightning Source LLC
Chambersburg PA
CBHW032015010726
47493CB00007B/2410